Limbo

The Last Humans: Book 2

Dima Zales

♠ Mozaika Publications ♠

This is a work of fiction. Names, characters, places, and incidents are either the product of the author's imagination or are used fictitiously, and any resemblance to actual persons, living or dead, business establishments, events, or locales is purely coincidental.

Published by Mozaika Publications, an imprint of Mozaika LLC.
www.mozaikallc.com

Cover by Najla Qamber Designs
www.najlaqamberdesigns.com

Edited by Elizabeth from arrowheadediting.wordpress.com and Mella Baxter

e-ISBN: 978-1-63142-142-6
Print ISBN: 978-1-63142-143-3

CHAPTER ONE

I'm walking in the desert, sun beaming down on my skin. In the distance, I see a blue shimmer. Is it a mirage? I run toward it, and the shimmer quickly turns into an endless blue ocean.

I feel elated. I always wanted to see the ocean.

Suddenly, a bikini-clad, pixie-haired figure appears in front of me and says, "I wasn't sure this would work, but I wanted to give it a shot. You're dreaming right now, but I need you to wake up."

Once I get over my surprise at her appearance, I realize she's right. On some level, I suspected I was dreaming. After all, there aren't any domes or barriers around me, and deep down I know that oceans and deserts don't exist in Oasis.

The realization wakes me with a start.

The Dorm lights are dimmed to a barely noticeable luminescence. This tells me it's not morning yet.

"I'm sorry about intruding on your dream," Phoe says. "I know it's still early, but this is urgent, and we need to talk."

Rubbing my eyes, I try to completely wake up.

Phoe is standing by my bed. Her usually smiling face is creased with worry lines. I have no way of knowing if she stood there like that all night. Actually, in the strictest sense of the word, she's not standing there. I can see her due to her mastery of the Augmented Reality interface. The real Phoe—the Artificial Intelligence that is the ship—is everywhere.

As I become more awake, the things I learned yesterday replay in my mind: the Quietude I got for asking too many questions in the wake of Mason's Forgetting, the Phoe-assisted escape from the Witch Prison, my shutting down of the Zoo, the IRES game that followed, running through the forest, flying on a disk, getting captured and almost killed, and playing the IRES game for the second and last time. More importantly, I remember the world-shattering revelations that followed, and this floods my mind with questions I didn't think of the other day. For example, if we're on a spaceship, where are we flying to? When will we get there? Why—

"I was actually working on answering those exact questions. Figuring out our location in the cosmos is one of my biggest priorities—after keeping us alive, that is." Phoe looks at the door warily before glancing back at me. "Unfortunately, I still lack the computational resources required to figure out where we are. However, I found out how we can get those resources. Except, as I was trying to say, survival comes first, and there's something you ought to see."

Her tone generates a rush of adrenaline that evaporates the last remnants of sleep from my brain. Automatically, I let the morning Cleaning take care of my teeth as I put my feet into my shoes and extend my hand for a bar of Food. A small end table with a cup of water is already there. Must be Phoe's work.

"Do I have time to eat or drink?" I mentally ask.

"Yes," she says. "The danger is not immediate. It's just something you have to see, and the sooner the better."

I bring up a Screen to check the time—5:45 a.m. I could've slept for at least two more hours. I stuff half of the Food bar into my mouth and chew it greedily while mumbling about unnecessary sleep deprivation.

"We got lucky," Phoe says, her gaze darting to the door again. "Their meeting happened in Virtual Reality space—my domain."

"Who are 'they'?" I mentally ask as I take a sip of water. "And what meeting?"

"You better see this with your own eyes." She bites her lip. "I don't trust language with something like this. It's a notoriously inaccurate mode of communication. Plus, I need to see if your assessment agrees with mine."

"Fine." I dry-swallow the rest of the Food and wash it down with water, trying to keep my eyes off her lips. "I'm ready."

"Your cave," Phoe says curtly. With a straight face, she makes the double-middle-figure gesture she invented for me to get into the virtual environment—as if I'd ever forget it.

I inwardly smile as I think of what Liam would say if he woke up and saw me do this gesture. He'd probably assume I was flipping him off.

"Now, Theo." Phoe's voice is a harsh whisper.

Phoe's body is no longer standing in front of me, so I do the gesture, aiming my middle fingers at where she *would* be standing were she still in the room.

If I had any remnants of sleepiness left, the 'white tunnel' experience would've definitively erased them.

Blinking rapidly, I look around my cave. There's a jar of rat poison to my right, and to my left is a plastic bathtub of something foul smelling—maybe hydrochloric acid.

"Is it okay if I immerse you in a Virtual Reality recording?" Phoe asks.

I look at where her voice came from, prepared to shield my eyes. The last time I saw Phoe in my cave, she was shiny with some kind of divine light.

"Yeah, you don't need to worry," she says, and I see that she looks exactly the way she did in the real world, except her blue eyes radiate concern. She moves her hands down her curves. "I'll take this shape when we're here, especially in light of what we're about to see."

I keep staring at her as she runs her hand through her hair, making her carefully engineered pixie cut into a genuine mess of spikes.

"So is it okay if I immerse you in this recording?" she prompts. "Do you consent to that?"

I blink. "Why not?"

"Well, I promised not to do anything to your mind without your permission. For you to see this, I'll have to patch you into—"

"Sure," I say as curiosity quickens my pulse. "Do whatever you need to do."

Phoe makes a gesture that resembles something an orchestra conductor might do. Instantly, my vision and hearing blur into white noise reminiscent of an ancient out-of-tune TV.

When the static clears from my senses, I'm no longer standing in my cave.

To the sounds of beautifully haunting music, I examine my surroundings.

The place looks like an ancient cathedral, except it's much larger. Even St. Peter's Basilica in Vatican

City, the biggest such structure I've read about, could fit inside this enormous hall many times over. The music vibrating through the air heightens my feeling of being small and insignificant.

"It's organ music." Phoe's tense voice echoes in my head. "Bach's *Toccata and Fugue in D minor* to be exact."

"So this is Virtual Reality, like my man cave?" I make a mental note to add this piece to my list of favorites and hope that my life gets normal enough for me to just listen to music at some point.

"What you're about to see originally happened in VR," Phoe says. "But it's different from your cave in that it's not 'live.' You're essentially seeing a surreptitious recording of the meeting. We're lucky they met here, where I could intercept it."

I scan the room for the source of the music. They used to have organ pipes in churches, but I don't find instruments of any kind or any obvious religious décor. Still, the music and the ultra-high ceilings evoke the sense that I'm in some strange place of worship.

"Well, that and the kneeling Jeremiah." Phoe's voice comes from a few feet away from where I'm standing.

I glance in that direction, but she's not there. Instead, I see what she's talking about: a white-robed, white-haired figure that almost blends in with the shiny, pale floor. Sitting by the large stage-like slab of marble, the figure is in a prayer-like position that looks like the child pose we learned in yoga. Though I can't see his face, I recognize Jeremiah instantly and feel violent urges toward him just as fast.

In my defense, the guy did torture me yesterday.

"Pay attention," Phoe says in a clipped tone. "Here comes the part you don't want to miss."

In sync with her words, a figure of pure light illuminates the middle of the platform.

The figure is so bright and intense that I'm forced to shield my eyes with my hands. This is like staring at the sun, if the sun had a humanoid shape. I close my eyes and remove my hands. I can still see the brightness through my eyelids.

"You may rise," the figure says, its voice sounding like it was crafted out of the organ music.

The brightness has dimmed, so I brave opening my eyes a sliver.

The figure is luminous but less so, and I can make out some details, like the fact that it's scantily clad in something resembling a loincloth—and that it's more accurate to say 'it' is a 'he,' at least judging by his muscular chest and shoulders. Of course, the human anatomy rationale breaks down when I factor in the creature's giant dove-like wings, with each feather radiating thousands of watts.

"Envoy," Jeremiah says once he's on his feet.

"Keeper," the being—the Envoy—replies in that same organ-sounding voice.

"You honor me with your presence," Jeremiah says, but his tone sounds more ceremonious than deferential.

"Ever so formal," says the Envoy and grants Jeremiah an angelic smile too beautiful for a male.

Jeremiah bows instead of replying.

"We'd like a report of recent goings-on," the Envoy says, his inhumanly ancient eyes sparkling like blue diamonds.

"What would you like to know, Envoy?" Jeremiah asks evenly. "There hasn't been much happening . . . at least nothing of note."

"Is that so?" The Envoy's beatific smile is gone.

"Well . . ." For the first time, Jeremiah sounds mildly wary. "We're fully prepared for the upcoming Birth Day. The babies in the Incubators will be born on schedule, and the celebratory preparations are on track. The new generation of the Elderly received instructions on what to expect and were briefed about the Test . . ."

As he speaks, the Envoy's features and the space surrounding him darken, as if he's absorbed all the light he was previously emitting. The frown is like a strange mask on his ethereal face.

Jeremiah takes a step back.

"Nothing else you want to discuss?" The Envoy's voice takes on those darker qualities that only organ pipes can produce. "Nothing to do with the Council?"

"I don't understand," Jeremiah says and audibly swallows. "What about the Council?"

"The Council meeting." The melody in the Envoy's voice grows increasingly frightening.

"What Council meeting?" Jeremiah's voice breaks. "I already reported on the last one . . ."

The Envoy's graceful hands squeeze into fists. There's something thunder-god-like about the being's eyes in that moment, causing me to wonder if he's about to smite Jeremiah with a bolt of lightning. The look he gives the old man is like those legendary ones the ancients wrote about—deadly. I'm shocked Jeremiah isn't a small pile of ash on the floor.

"I'd like to employ the Lens of Truth to ask my next question." The Envoy's musical voice hits its deepest bass note yet. "You remember what *that* entails?"

"You think I—" Blood leaves Jeremiah's face, allowing him to blend in with the white marble floor. Then, as if thinking better of it, he says hastily, "Yes, of course." Jeremiah puts his hand on his chest solemnly. "I consent to the Lens of Truth and swear to tell the truth and nothing but the truth."

As Jeremiah says the last word, his hand falls limply to his side, and his eyes glaze over.

"Do you remember the Council meeting that happened mere hours ago?" the Envoy asks.

"I do not," Jeremiah says in a zombie-like tone.

The Envoy's fists unclench, his expression changing to one of confusion. "Has anything out of the ordinary happened since your last report?"

"No," Jeremiah says. "The incident with Mason was the last noteworthy event, and that was concluded and reported on already."

"Have you ever considered betraying your duty as the Keeper of Information?" The Envoy folds his wings around his body the way someone would a cape. "Have you ever considered using Forgetting on yourself, even though you ought not to?"

"No . . . and no." Jeremiah's voice is unnerving in its complete lack of emotion. "I have not Forgotten anything since I took over as the Keeper."

"Except that if you did, you wouldn't be lying," the Envoy says. His melodious voice sounds disappointed. "A lie is not a lie if you don't know you're lying."

Jeremiah stares at the being. I guess whatever this 'Lens of Truth' state is, when under it, Jeremiah needs to be asked a question if he is to respond.

"Are you aware that every formal Council meeting is automatically reported to us?" the Envoy asks.

Seems he also realized the need to pose a question.

"Yes." Jeremiah's face is completely blank.

"So, without an actual Council meeting, can you think of any other reason why we would receive such an automated report?"

"No."

The Envoy gestures at Jeremiah in a hurried, jerky motion, and the old man's eyes return to normal. I didn't think he could get paler, but he manages it. His skin is almost translucent, with blue veins visible on his temples.

"Do you see?" the Envoy asks solemnly. "Do you see the enormity of it?"

"I do," Jeremiah says, his lips quivering. "Someone made *me* Forget."

CHAPTER TWO

The scene stops. The Envoy was about to say something, but his mouth is frozen mid-sentence.

Phoe appears in front of me. Her fingers look like they just completed a flicking gesture.

"What you heard isn't the worst of it." Her forehead is wrinkled in a frown. "I just wanted to pause the proceedings because your neural patterns were worrying me."

"Oh? It's my brain chemistry that worries you?" My voice echoes through the virtual cathedral. Taking a couple of steps toward the marble stage, I point at the winged creature. "Shouldn't *this* worry you?"

"Obviously everything worries me," Phoe says, her frown deepening. "It's just that their conversation already happened and nothing can be done about *that,* while I can modulate your wellbeing by giving you this shocking information slowly."

"Enough worrying about *me,*" I say, jumping onto the platform. Walking over to the winged creature, I ask, "What or who is this?" Up close, the details of his impressive musculature become more apparent; he could easily make a Greek sculpture feel inadequate.

"I don't know who or what he is." Her response is barely audible.

"What do you mean you don't know?" I back away from the frozen figure as though Phoe's lack of knowledge will make him come to life. "Don't you usually know everything?"

"Yet I have no clue." She looks down at the floor. "Not for lack of trying, I assure you."

"Okay," I say slowly. "If *I* had to guess, I'd say he's an AI . . . like you." I remember how she looked all godlike when she gained the IRES game's resources.

"I don't know about that." She crosses her arms and rubs her shoulders slowly.

"Well, look at it logically," I say, ignoring her discomfort. "As far as you know, do any Youths, Adults, or Elderly have your capabilities?"

As expected, she shakes her head.

I try to catch her gaze. "Doesn't that leave AI as the only possibility?"

"I don't know." Phoe evades my stare. "My memory isn't perfect. It won't be even close to perfect until I can completely recover all my computing resources, but as far as I know, no AI should be on this voyage besides me."

"Well, can this somehow be you?" I suggest. "Another aspect of you that gained resources and consciousness at some point, the way you did, and then proceeded to develop independently?"

A medley of emotions flits across her face as she turns to look at Jeremiah. "I don't think that's possible," she says, staring at the old man's figure. "Plus, there's evidence against that idea."

"You don't sound too certain," I think, partly to myself but mostly for her benefit.

She doesn't respond, so I say out loud, "Can't you use your hacking skills to figure this out?"

Phoe turns back to me. "This cathedral is located in a DMZ of sorts. It took a lot of effort for me to tap into it. I was lucky I got into it at all. But when I tried to trace his origin"—she points at the Envoy—"no matter how hard I tried, I couldn't. I reached an impenetrable Firewall that blocked me from accessing a large chunk of the overall computing resources. And I don't mean I just can't use them. I can't even fathom what's there. And he clearly exists in that unreachable region."

"What's a DMZ?" I ask. "And for that matter, what's a Firewall?"

"Demilitarized Zone—DMZ for short—was an ancient computing term," Phoe says. "Think of it as a layer of security against hacking that lies between systems that aren't secured and systems that are heavily secured. A Firewall is another measure of security, one between the DMZ and whatever it is you're trying to hack. It's the Firewall that has me baffled, but none of this should be the focus of our conversation. I think we should be discussing the mess we've gotten ourselves into."

I nod, letting go of the mystery of the Envoy's identity for now to focus on the meaning of his conversation with Jeremiah.

Yesterday, Fiona, one of the Elderly, called a Council meeting to object to Jeremiah's method of questioning me (via torture). The meeting took place but didn't really change anything. The Council decided to allow Jeremiah to do what he wanted.

After I beat the IRES game and Phoe got the resources she needed, she was able to make everyone Forget I was ever in trouble, which means that Jeremiah can no longer recall the 'should we torture Theo?' Council meeting. Unfortunately for us, it seems this Envoy was notified that the cursed meeting was scheduled. Thanks to that, the Envoy knows that a Forgetting happened.

"Yes, your assessment agrees with mine," Phoe says as a voice in my head. "And before you ask your next question, let me show you this."

Phoe flicks her fingers, and the conversation between Jeremiah and the Envoy speeds up. Their lips move like leaves in a tornado, and their voices sound high-pitched. The effect would be comical if it weren't for the bits and pieces of conversation I catch—information that confirms what I've already deduced. They know that Jeremiah's brain was somehow tampered with, which should be impossible given his role as the Keeper of Information.

Phoe returns the recording to normal speed as Jeremiah asks, "Can you undo the Forgetting? Return to me what I have lost?"

"No," the Envoy responds, the melody of his voice brooding. "I can't recover your memories, but we can monitor you and the Council going forward. If you're made to Forget again, I should be able to learn who was behind this atrocity."

Phoe snaps her fingers again, and the scene pauses.

I exhale the breath I was holding in. The point the Envoy made about whether he can undo Forgetting is a question that goes to the core of my anxiety.

"That is one bit of evidence that proves this Envoy isn't *me,* assuming you still needed reassurance on that front," Phoe says. "I *can* undo a Forgetting, if I choose to do so."

"Well, he could be lying," I begin to say but stop. "No, he wouldn't have a good reason to lie about that." I inhale. "I'm glad he isn't you. If he were you and could undo Forgetting, that would be a disaster. I mean, if Jeremiah recalled what happened, the Guards would be on their way to get me as we speak."

"No." Phoe rubs the heel of her palm against her chest. "*The Guards* aren't on their way to get you . . ."

I look at her questioningly, and she flicks her fingers again.

The scene speeds up once more, then slows as the Envoy says, "Logic would dictate that you start your investigation with the last Forgetting." He wrinkles his nose. "The unfortunate case of that insane Youth, Mason."

Without my being conscious of what I'm doing, my hand strikes the Envoy in the face, but the punch doesn't connect. Instead, my fist goes through the Envoy's face. I should've guessed it would, since I'm inside of a recording.

Phoe pauses the conversation. "I don't blame you for trying to smack him," she says. "If I could punch this winged prick, I would."

I take a couple of calming breaths and say, "Investigating Mason would lead them to me."

"Yes." Phoe's blue eyes are pools of worry. "And there's this."

She fast-forwards the conversation until Jeremiah says, "I'd like to be granted the Lens of Truth for this investigation."

Phoe pauses the recording again and interjects, "In case you missed it, the Lens of Truth is what the Envoy used to make Jeremiah answer his questions earlier. I believe it's a neural lie detection algorithm of some kind."

She continues the recording.

The Envoy looks thoughtful for a moment, then decisively says, "All right. You and Fiona will be granted the Lens of Truth for the duration of this investigation."

"Fiona?" There's a note of agitation in Jeremiah's voice.

"Yes," the Envoy replies, watching Jeremiah intently.

"But she's the reason I requested the Lens of Truth to begin with." Jeremiah's jaw tightens. "She's the very person I want to question first."

"That would be completely out of the question," the Envoy says, his voice so forceful it reverberates in my belly. "I will not allow you to turn this quagmire into a platform for petty political squabbles." He shakes his index finger at Jeremiah. "Fiona is a capable Councilwoman, and if something were to happen to you"—there's a threatening undertone to the Envoy's words—"she'd succeed you as the Keeper."

For a moment, Jeremiah looks like he was struck. He seems to be considering whether to talk back. Either his fear or respect wins out, because he says, "I understand, Envoy. The honorable Fiona and I will take your gift and investigate."

For the first time since the Forgetting issue came up, the Envoy looks pleased. I guess pairing Jeremiah with Fiona was some kind of test, and Jeremiah passed.

"You'll start with Mason's cohorts and work your way up to the Instructors." The Envoy's voice is a calmer melody. "If the Lens needs to be used on any of the Elderly, I want to be notified about it first."

"As you wish," Jeremiah says, and his mouth freezes.

I look at Phoe, who's flicked her fingers again.

Though I expected the Envoy to say something along those lines, now it's official. I'm definitely one of Mason's cohorts.

Phoe and I stand there in silence. Then she looks me in the eye and says, "We're done here. Let's go back to the real world."

I open my mouth to launch into a torrent of objections, but Phoe is no longer in the room.

I take one last look at the mystery AI, or whatever the Envoy is, and signal to leave the VR, showing one middle finger to Jeremiah and the other to the winged creature.

The white tunnel swirls me back to my man cave, and I repeat the gesture. Another white whirlwind later, I find myself back on my bed in the real world.

Phoe is still standing above me. When she sees me open my eyes, she sighs deeply, and a distant expression appears on her face.

"So," I say, breaking the silence, "they'll investigate me using that Lens of Truth."

"Most likely, yes," Phoe says, but she sounds distracted. "Jeremiah just called upon the Council to discuss it, so I suggest we wait until that meeting is over before we decide what to do next."

"But—"

"I mean it. We need to know all the variables."

"And you can eavesdrop on their meeting?" I frown. "Isn't it risky, given the Envoy situation?"

"So long as I stay out of their minds, I shouldn't be detected. Hopefully."

"I guess it's worth the risk." I get up from the bed. "We have to know how deep this goes."

"Exactly." She looks distant again. "It's going to happen in about twenty minutes. We can wait that long."

"Okay," I subvocalize. "In the meantime, I think I need some fresh air."

"Good idea," Phoe says and heads for the door.

We're both pretty quiet as we make our way out of the Dorm building.

When we get outside, we're greeted by the rising sun.

"Beautiful, isn't it?" Phoe says.

I'm not sure if she's talking about the sunrise or how it's reflecting off the dew on the grass, but she's right. It's been ages since I've woken up this early, and I guess I was missing out. Even knowing that the sun isn't real, that we're in space surrounded by stars, doesn't detract from its beauty.

I walk down the green walkway and notice Youths who are already awake. To my right, a couple of boys are meditating. To my left, two girls are practicing yoga.

When I turn the corner, heading toward the soccer field, a Youth inserts himself in my path. I'm so lost in thought that it takes me a moment to realize it's Owen. What the hell is *he* doing awake at this unreasonably early hour? Somehow, I doubt he got up to meditate.

When he sees I've spotted him, he walks toward me.

Not in the mood for his shenanigans, I attempt to get past him by stepping right.

He steps to his left, once again blocking my path.

I automatically step to the left.

He moves to the right this time. Clearly, he's trying to get in my way.

I stop and say, "What do you want?"

"Oh, I didn't even notice you there, Why-Odor," Owen says in his hyena-like tone. "If you want to dance, why don't you just ask me?"

"I'm not in the mood for your shit," I say. The intensity in my voice, as well as my blatant breaking of the vulgarity rules, makes Owen take a slight step back.

Unfortunately, he recovers quickly and says, "Well, I am in the mood for a chat." He looks around to make sure no one can overhear him, sees that we're alone, and quietly adds, "So who gives a shit what you want?"

"I'll give you two seconds to get out of my way," I say as evenly as I can, given the tension of the morning thus far. "One."

"Theo, don't," Phoe whispers.

"Fuck you," Owen replies and puffs out his chest, looking like a weird hyena-peacock hybrid.

"Wrong answer," I think, and without saying a word, I do something I've only done once in the IRES simulation.

I ball my hand into a fist and punch Owen in the jaw.

CHAPTER THREE

I expect Owen to raise his fists and fight back, like in the IRES game. To be honest, I'm hoping he'll give me a reason to hit him again.

He doesn't raise his fists. He just stands there, looking as stunned as a cartoon character that ran off a cliff.

Then, to my surprise, Owen gracelessly collapses.

"Dude?" I say, looking down at him. "Owen?"

He doesn't reply.

I think I knocked him out, like an ancient boxer.

"Is he okay?" I ask Phoe.

With a flick of her wrist, Phoe brings up a Screen.

I see vitals on the screen and assume they're Owen's. They look normal, but I wait for her to answer.

"Yes, he's fine," she says and shakes her head. "I didn't expect you to do that."

"I'm sorry," I say, half to her and half to the unconscious Owen. "I'm not used to having so much pent-up emotion." I rub my aching knuckles with my left hand. "I had no idea my punch would be *that* effective."

"Well . . ." Phoe clears her throat. "It normally wouldn't be, but I did something to a group of nanos in your body while you were sleeping, and this might be a tiny side effect of that." She gives me a weak smile. "I've been meaning to tell you about it."

"What?" The hair on the back of my neck rises.

"There's nothing to be concerned about." Phoe's smile wanes. "Remember how much interest you showed in the rejuvenation nanos that are dormant in your body? Well, once you went to sleep, I scanned you with my newly enhanced senses, and I found many more nanos that are meant to be generally beneficial. They also seem to have been developed before Oasis was formed, and like the longevity-enhancing rejuvenation nanos, it looks like their effects were never turned on." She scratches her cheek. "I examined the ones that were safe and simple in their operations, and when I felt confident, I turned one of them on. It seemed like such a terrible waste of potential . . ."

As she speaks, I feel blood drain from my face. "You said you wouldn't mess with me without my permission."

"No." She steps backward. "I said I wouldn't tamper with your mind. What I enabled has nothing to do with your brain. Well, not exactly, anyway. I guess it gives your brain steady oxygen." She scratches her neck this time. "Basically, what I did will make your body work more efficiently. This nano does what a regular red blood cell does, only better."

I look at her, unblinking, debating whether she's kidding around with this nonchalant discussion of manipulating frightening ancient technology *inside my body*. I vaguely recall reading that red blood cells carry oxygen and take carbon dioxide out.

"Exactly." Phoe seems to be examining my shoes. "These devices are called Respirocytes. They work better than red blood cells ever could. With them enabled, you should be able to survive for hours without breathing. They'll allow you to run much easier and sprint longer distances without getting out of breath. That's why I took the liberty of activating them, given all that running you did yesterday. I thought you'd be pleased."

I remember all my huffing and puffing yesterday, and some of my anxiety gives way to curiosity. Not needing to breathe for hours? That's impossible.

"There you go," Phoe says, her smile reappearing as she looks up at me. "That's the spirit. Respirocyte is the earliest nanocyte ever invented. Its design was put forth as early as the late twentieth century. The ones in your body were simple enough in construction and function that I could verify they were safe beyond a shadow of doubt, even with my limited resources. I never would've enabled them otherwise."

"Fine," I subvocalize. "Just ask me before you enable anything else next time."

"Deal," Phoe says. Then she adds quickly, "With the exception of special situations, such as when you're in mortal danger and enabling something might save your life."

"Agreed," I subvocalize and look back at the unconscious Owen. "Now can you explain to me how the extra oxygen made me stronger?"

"Oxygen definitely makes your muscles perform better, though I didn't think the effect would be *that* significant." She looks at Owen's vitals again. "It is conceivable that, in addition to your punch, he also lost consciousness due to shock. After all, he probably hasn't been hit in over a decade, if ever—"

"Oh, he's been hit. I remember when Liam punched him in kindergarten." I smile at the memory. "He didn't get knocked out, but he did cry—profusely."

"There you go." Mirth enters Phoe's gaze. "This confirms my theory that bullies are secretly pussies." She glances down at Owen. "And sometimes not so secretly."

Though I'm still a little mad at her, I can't help but chuckle.

I gesture to snap a photo of Owen in his unconscious condition and bring it up on my Screen. I debate sending it to Liam but decide against it. The Adults could easily intercept and correctly interpret what happened, which would lead to a Quietude of legendary proportions.

"They can even access it this way," Phoe says.

"Can you delete it then?" I subvocalize.

"You never actually took the picture." She winks. "I intercepted the command and put that image on your Screen locally."

"Devious," I subvocalize and dismiss my Screen.

She stands there looking smug, and I turn my attention inward.

If what Phoe said is true and I really *can* survive for hours without breathing, I should be able to hold my breath beyond my previous record of fifty seconds.

I hold my breath to put her words to the test.

At first it feels like any other time I've held my breath—not bothersome at the beginning.

Emboldened, I count Theodores: *one Theodore, two Theodores, three . . .*

I know from prior experience that ten seconds is when a slight discomfort usually begins.

This time, however, it doesn't. I feel exactly the way I did on the first second.

After thirty seconds, I still don't feel any unease.

After sixty Theodores, my mood improves with every passing second.

"I'm glad you finally appreciate my gift." A hint of mockery dances in Phoe's voice. "But you didn't knock him out strongly enough to hang out here much longer. At this point, I'm preventing him from getting up using methods I'd rather *not* use, given all the unwanted attention. I also don't consider it very ethical to be doing this, even if it's Owen we're talking about."

"Will you make him Forget?" I pointedly keep holding my breath.

"I already did," Phoe says. "If you really want to test the Respirocytes, you should sprint to your favorite spot while holding your breath."

"That's a great idea," I think.

"The only type of ideas I get." She grins, turns her back to me, and runs.

Resisting the temptation to give Owen's butt a kick, I follow her.

Phoe runs fast, but I keep up. In a few moments, I'm approaching my full-on sprinting speed.

I take long strides and focus on my breath. Minutes pass, and I don't feel the need to breathe. A few more minutes later, there still isn't a hint of me running out of breath. As I run, pure joy replaces my initial concerns and my grievances with Phoe. Every millisecond is identical to that very first rush I got when I started sprinting. And it's not just not needing to breathe that's different. Running is subtly easier. My muscles seem to recover faster from the exertion.

"If you inhale, they'll recover even faster," Phoe says over her shoulder. "Though I believe you should be able to keep this up for a while."

I exhale and instantly inhale again, then hold my breath for another minute as I run.

"I should've run faster to test your limits," Phoe says when we reach the bushes that signal the Edge of Oasis.

She walks through them and I follow, still holding that last breath.

"Why do we have these nanos if we don't use them?" I think at Phoe.

"They're embedded into the embryos that become citizens of Oasis," she responds in my head. "Like I told you before, since the Forebears eliminated natural reproduction along with sex, all Oasis babies result from embryos that came from Earth, during a time when not using this technology in a baby was considered criminally negligent. The Elderly must somehow disable and control these nanos. When I get my hands on that process, we might allow a new generation to be born the way they should've been."

I digest what she said as I look at the strange skies. Here, there are stars where the Goo used to be, stars that meet the morning sky where the sun is still coming up. Augmented Reality manages to blend and smooth the two impossible views together. The blue sky has a couple of stars near the horizon, then it darkens gradually, going fully black where the Goo would be. I breathe out audibly in awe. This view will take a long time to get used to.

My lungs nearly empty, I force myself to exhale some more, testing what will happen. Nothing really does, and I'm able to stay this way, though holding the 'out' breath while my lungs are empty feels unpleasant. I allow my body to inhale normally, then exhale, and repeat the cycle a few times. When my breathing becomes subconscious again, I subvocalize, "Okay, Phoe. I officially forgive you. That was really cool."

She looks back at me with a strange mix of pity and worry. "You can be such a kid sometimes." She pauses, then adds softly, "I regret I got you involved in all this."

Her seriousness reminds me of the things I put out of my mind for the last few minutes. "I'm glad you got me involved," I subvocalize and realize I actually mean it. "I'm glad I know you. I'd always rather know the truth."

I look at the stars again, thinking of what lies out there.

"I so desperately want to figure out where we are," Phoe says, moving to stand next to me. She looks at the stars with such longing that I feel an odd ache in my chest.

"You couldn't locate us even with your new resources?" I ask quietly.

"Right, I couldn't. But I did have a plan as to how to acquire the necessary resources." Phoe's gaze is distant, and her voice sounds wistful.

"You did?"

"Yes, but it's not important now." She forces a smile to her lips.

"I'd like to hear about it anyway," I think. Then I can't help but add, "Along with anything else you might have done to the technology in my body."

"I didn't do anything else to you, I swear," she says, turning to look at me. "Regarding my plan, do you remember the Test Jeremiah mentioned at the very beginning of his conversation with the Envoy?"

"Vaguely." I sit down on the grass.

"Well, when I intercepted their conversation, it wasn't the first time I'd heard of this Test." She sits next to me, and thanks to the tactile Augmented Reality, her leg brushes against mine. "This Test was on my radar soon after you fell asleep last night."

"He said something about the new generation of the Elderly and Birth Day," I subvocalize, pulling my feet toward me. "It sounds like those rumors you hear about the exit exam that Youths take on our fortieth Birth Day. They say it's so the Adults can see what our jobs will be once we join them."

"Yes, and they're not rumors." She scoots sideways so she's closer to me. "Youths take an aptitude-and-interests Test. It's nothing sinister, just a way to figure out what you want to do with yourself as an Adult. The Elderly Test is a little more mysterious. I don't know what its actual purpose is—probably also to test aptitude for something—but the interesting thing about it is that it uses technology similar to the IRES game, which is how it got on my to-deal-with list."

"How similar?" My pulse accelerates. "You don't want me to beat something like that cursed game again, do you?" The memories of falling from the tower and fighting cyborg-Jeremiah flit through my mind.

"You know I do, or else I wouldn't have brought it up, but I don't think the Test will be as disturbing as the game was," Phoe says. "The only thing they have in common is the ultra-realistic immersion you'll experience and that it's tailored to each user's brain. Whatever the Test's purpose is, given that it's something the Adults take as a prelude to becoming a member of the Elderly, we can be sure it will *not* be entertaining."

I shake my head at her reminder that the game, with all its unpleasantness, was designed with entertainment in mind. But then, what else would you expect from the ancients? They were insane enough to jump out of airplanes, handing their lives over to contraptions made out of fabric. I have a very hard time seeing anyone in Oasis wanting to put Adults through a game like that to initiate them as the Elderly.

A new realization takes my anxiety in a different direction, and I subvocalize, "If it's a Test only Adults are supposed to take, how can I take it? Wouldn't they notice something like that?" I turn my whole body toward Phoe. "Also, if I'm supposed to bring this Test down the way I did with the IRES game, wouldn't the Elderly notice that? Wouldn't they get suspicious? First the Zoo shuts down, then this?"

"We're still talking hypothetically?"

"Right."

"Well then, let me answer the easy questions first." Phoe also turns so we're facing each other. "If you're the last person to take the Test this Birth Day, my hope is that no one will notice its absence for a year, until the next Birth Day, which might as well be an eternity from now as far as I'm concerned. I can figure something out by the time they need to take the Test again. Also, I didn't get a chance to tell you this, but I brought the Zoo back online to make sure no one noticed it was gone, although that further reduced my resources and increased the need for this Test."

"Okay." I digest that as I hold her gaze. "What about the not-so-easy questions?"

"I had a very clever scheme in mind, something that can only be done on Birth Day." Phoe smiles mischievously. "When their systems update everyone's ages, I was going to tweak yours so that instead of twenty-four, you'd turn the ripe age of ninety." She puts her palm out, silencing my upcoming objections. "I was going to dedicate part of myself to monitoring anyone accessing your age statistics. If and when anyone tries to look at your age, that part of me would make sure they saw your real age, twenty-four. That wouldn't require any

Augmented Reality manipulation. I would simply trick the Screen of whoever—"

"Okay," I subvocalize slowly. "So you have a way to let me take the Test."

"Right."

"And you need it gone so you can get more resources?"

"Exactly."

"To figure out where we are—where *you* are, as in the ship?"

"That," she says, "and our destination. I want to know where we're flying to."

I feel gooseflesh rise on my arms. It's the same reaction I get whenever I let myself think about the idea that we're flying someplace specific.

"Yeah," Phoe says, the awe in her voice echoing my state of mind. "We could be traveling to settle on some new, Earth-like planet. Lots of evidence, like that stash of embryos, points to that possibility."

An Earth-like planet.

I remember my earlier dream. It's a possibility so wonderful I'm afraid to hope. Running for miles and miles without the Barrier of the Dome to stop me would literally be a dream come true.

"What about Earth?" I think. "Is there any chance we could go back?"

"We could, in theory at least," Phoe says. "We got from there to here, so we should be able to get back. But, Theo, going back there would be a rather radical scenario."

"Because of the technological advances?"

"Yes." Her voice is soft. "I wasn't brought up to be a Luddite the way you were, and even I find the idea of Earth overwhelming."

Phoe told me earlier that Earth might, by this point, be a planet that is itself intelligent—whatever that means. The whole solar system could be sentient, she said. Meeting something like that sounds both frightening and wondrous. If we are truly mortal—an idea I'm still keeping locked in a small box somewhere in my mind—then I want to see what's happened on Earth before I die.

"I'm glad you feel that way," Phoe replies as a thought. "Because if anyone could make that happen, it would be me."

"To that end, maybe we can still implement your scheme?" I mentally ask. "Once we get out of this Envoy mess?"

Phoe raises her index finger to her mouth in a 'be silent' sign, which is funny since I was thinking, not talking, so she should be putting her finger to her temple. For a second, her eyes get a distant look before focusing again.

"They're about to have that Council meeting," she says.

She flicks her arm and a large Screen appears in front of us.

On the Screen is a spacious room with a bunch of white-haired Elderly sitting on ancient, throne-looking chairs.

Jeremiah is the only one who's standing.

To his right is Fiona, the woman who stood up for me yesterday. Every other Elderly looks completely unfamiliar.

"Ladies and Gentlemen of the Council," Jeremiah says, his face a stony mask. "There's a dire situation you need to be made aware of."

CHAPTER FOUR

The twelve Council members wear a mixture of worried and curious expressions. Fiona and four other women appear to have fallen on the curious end of the spectrum, and so do five of the men. The rest look concerned.

Jeremiah examines everyone's faces. I guess he still suspects one of them of causing the Forgetting, despite the Envoy's position on the matter. Or, as the Envoy insinuated, perhaps Jeremiah is looking for a way to use this situation to advance his political agenda. Judging by the way Fiona confronted him yesterday, Jeremiah and Fiona seem to be at philosophical and political odds.

Having completed his examination, Jeremiah says, "An unauthorized Forgetting was perpetrated."

The silence in the Council room is absolute, their faces almost comical in their shades of shock.

"That's impossible," a younger-looking man says. "It can't even—"

"It's fact." Jeremiah plants his feet in a wide stance. "The Envoy has informed me."

The room erupts in incredulous whispers.

"How convenient," Fiona says, getting up from her chair, "given that you're the only one with access to the Envoy."

Jeremiah bares his yellowish-gray teeth in a smile that lacks even a hint of warmth. "Would *you* like to meet the Envoy?"

Fiona visibly pales, sits back down, and stays quiet.

I guess meeting the Envoy is considered a scary proposition—something I take note of.

"I apologize for my outburst," Jeremiah says to Fiona in a completely unapologetic tone. "The Envoy, in his wisdom, included you in the forthcoming investigation, so if you need proof of my words, know that he endowed you with the Lens of Truth."

The murmurs turn into shocked exclamations.

Fiona whispers something to a thin man sitting next to her, and Jeremiah says, "If you're testing it on Vincent, don't. We are to start our investigation with Youths, followed by Adults. If we need to question any of the Elderly"—he gives the rest of the Council a threatening glance—"I will have to consult with the Envoy again."

"I see," Fiona says, her slender fingers twitching at her sides. "I guess I can test it later."

Jeremiah gives her a contemptuous look. "Why would I lie about something so easily verifiable?" When Fiona shrugs, he says, "I also wouldn't recommend using this power idly. It was granted to us for a specific purpose, and that is to investigate the atrocity committed against everyone here." He sweeps his hand around the circle of the Elderly.

"Committed against *you*," says Vincent, the emaciated man Fiona just whispered to. "The rest of us have been through a Forgetting many times."

Jeremiah's posture stiffens. "You never agreed to Forget *this*. There's a Council meeting missing from our minds, and who knows what else. There was no psychological benefit to this Forgetting. It was done with malicious intent."

Every Council member speaks at once. In the cacophony, I make out questions along the lines of "How can that be?" and "Who could even do such a thing?"

"I will have order in the Council," Jeremiah says, raising his voice above all others. "You are acting like a bunch of Youths."

The noise quiets down.

"Now." Jeremiah scowls. "I think you understand the severity of this situation. The only people who have the power of Forgetting are in this room, yet somehow, *we* were the targets."

Jeremiah pauses for dramatic effect, and it works. Everyone looks at him with bated breath. Vincent literally slides to the edge of his seat. Even Fiona looks subdued and respectful.

"The Envoy nominated me and Fiona to lead the investigation into this dire matter," Jeremiah says. "We are to start with . . . well, this is where things get tricky, as we are getting into matters I cannot recall." He pinches the loose skin on his neck. "There was an unfortunate situation where a Youth was Forgotten two days ago, and there's a chance that this rather rare event is somehow related to our predicament."

The noise is back.

Fiona looks around at her fellow Council members and speaks up, raising her voice to be heard over everyone's mumbling. "I have no doubt you're telling the truth, Jeremiah, but you have to understand how difficult it is for us to believe that a Youth had to be Forgotten."

"I can't even imagine what you're feeling, but I do envy you all." Jeremiah looks genuinely sad as he says this. "I carry the burden of remembering these tragedies. If it were not necessary, I would not have brought it up, but there's no other way for us to discuss the Envoy's plan."

"What is the Envoy's plan?" Vincent is a millimeter away from slipping off his chair.

"Fiona and I will interview everyone who knew this unfortunate Youth," Jeremiah says. "That is, after I figure out who his friends and enemies were."

"How will you do that?" Fiona tilts her head to the side. "Wasn't the information irrevocably lost during the Forgetting?"

Phoe and I exchange glances.

I didn't even think of this, but it makes sense. If Mason wasn't mentioned anywhere, then getting a list of his friends is impossible.

Jeremiah frowns. "The Keepers have their own private, unaltered archives," he says with evident reluctance. "And if you"—he stares at Fiona—"are willing to undergo Forgetting after this matter is finished, I could give you access to them to aid in this investigation."

Phoe tenses. She must've hoped they didn't have unaltered archives. Then she sighs and says as a thought in my mind, "At least this gives me a valuable resource."

"Let me listen to them," I think back and concentrate on the Screen, where Fiona has already said a few words I missed.

"—would submit to a Forgetting if the good of Oasis required it," Fiona says and glances around the group uneasily. "I will do whatever I can to assist this investigation."

"It's settled then," Jeremiah says. "The rest of you, after all this is done, will have the luxury of Forgetting that a Youth suffered such an unpleasant fate. Now—"

"I'm sorry, Keeper," says a round-faced old woman. "Are you planning to work on this immediately?"

"Of course," Jeremiah says with a note of kindness in his voice. This must be a woman he likes.

"And you'll need Fiona?"

"Obviously." Jeremiah's kindness slips toward annoyance.

"It's just that"—the old woman reddens—"we're about to get a new crop of newborns on Birth Day. It's a lot of work. Plus we're moving the older youngsters to the Youth section, and there are the celebrations themselves . . ." Her voice trails off.

Jeremiah looks at the woman, then at the rest of the Council members, and finally at Fiona.

Fiona doesn't look like she noticed his stare or heard the round-faced woman's complaints. She appears lost in thought.

"I have a question too," Vincent says. "How can you and Fiona interview Youths? Will you bring them here and make them Forget it ever happened? They aren't supposed to see any signs of aging."

"That's easy enough," a younger-looking Elderly says. "Fiona and Jeremiah can dress as Guards. It's what—"

"I'm sorry," Fiona interrupts. "There's a thought I can't shake, and please forgive me if I'm being paranoid, but to paraphrase what Jeremiah said at the beginning of this meeting: if someone made us Forget, wouldn't the most logical person be one of us?"

She looks around the room.

The rest of the Council members look at each other warily.

"The Envoy wants us to start with people outside the Elderly," Jeremiah says. "So I assume he has reasons to—"

"And that may be a prudent approach," Fiona says, "but I think it might not hurt to take a precaution or two anyway. I propose that Jeremiah and I continue discussing this matter privately."

"I think that's a great idea," Jeremiah says and gives Fiona the sullen look of someone who wishes the idea had been his. "But we'll have to put it to a vote, since the rest of the Council will be deprived of information that is their due."

"Of course," Fiona says and gives Jeremiah a sharp smile. "All in favor of *discretion,* please raise your hands."

She raises her hand. Jeremiah does the same.

Everyone else's hands follow. Those two obviously wield all the power in the room. The Envoy was clever to force their alliance, which sucks all the more for me.

"All right then," Jeremiah says. "Going forward, Fiona and I will discuss this matter privately. Now we can talk about other matters, including the Birth Day celebrations." He gives the round-faced woman a fake-looking smile.

The woman takes his smile at face value and launches into a laundry list of activities that need to be done for the big day.

Halfway through it, Phoe closes the Screen and says, "Part of me is still monitoring their conversation. If they talk about anything of note, I'll tell you."

I audibly let out a breath I inadvertently kept in—probably throughout the whole Council meeting.

"Can I panic *now?*" I'm so upset I say the words out loud. Subvocally, I add, "Do we have all the facts?"

It's only when I finish speaking that I notice how pale Phoe is.

"Yes," she says softly. "*Now* we can panic."

CHAPTER FIVE

I jump to my feet, unable to sit still.

Phoe gets up too.

"I didn't know." Phoe twists her hands together. "I didn't know about the unaltered archives."

"But now that you do, can you somehow make it so they can't connect me to Mason?" I take a step toward her. "Please, tell me you can."

"I have no idea where this archive is, and I've been searching for it since Jeremiah mentioned it. With my new resources, a few seconds is a long time." She doesn't meet my gaze. "On the bright side, once they access it, things might change, unless, like the Envoy, it's behind that cursed Firewall."

I pace back and forth for a while, and she just watches me.

"What do we do, Phoe?" I subvocalize after a minute. "They might find out I was Mason's friend and come interrogate me at any moment."

"They're still in the meeting. Afterwards, it might take them a while to scan through those secret archives." Stepping toward me, Phoe catches my forearm. "On top of that, even now, that round-faced woman is persuading them to help with the Birth Day chores."

"Okay, so I have two days instead of one." I pull away and make another circle around her. "The situation is still pretty screwed up."

Phoe nods, her expression tense.

"Can't you think of anything we can do?" I ask, stopping to take in a few deep breaths. Respirocytes don't seem to negatively affect the relaxation the exercise brings me, which is good.

"I've thought of a multitude of plans," Phoe says, "but all of them have flaws."

I resume pacing a bit slower. This time it's my mind that's racing and not my legs. An idea is forming, but it's pretty insane.

"Would that Lens of Truth make me answer all of Jeremiah's questions truthfully? Even though you protected my brain from mind control earlier?" I subvocalize, figuring that before I state my crazy plan, I should verify that I'm as deeply in shit as I think I am. "I wouldn't be able to lie . . . even to protect you?"

"I'm sorry, Theo, but I don't think the protection I gave you earlier would work against this, and if I tried to counter it at this point, I might as well announce my existence to them." Phoe frowns in concentration. "That is, assuming I figure out exactly how it works, which I think I could. Even the ancients had lie detection technology, and if I read up on its evolution over the years—"

"Never mind the technical details," I think and stop in front of her. "You said you could undo a Forgetting, right?"

"Yes," she says.

"Okay. Remember when the Envoy said that if Jeremiah really did make himself Forget, he wouldn't have been lying under the Lens of Truth, even if he actually was lying?" I run my hands through my hair and wait for her to nod. "So, my idea is this: you make *me* Forget, so that when they eventually ask me questions as part of this investigation, I'll honestly say I don't know anything. Then, later, you can undo the Forgetting and—"

"You think this wasn't one of the first solutions I thought about?" Phoe gently touches my elbow. "You haven't fully considered what you're asking. You would Forget *me.* You would Forget Mason. You would Forget—"

"I obviously don't want to do this." I resume pacing circles around her. "I just don't see any other options. If you mess with their minds, the Envoy will know. If I'm caught lying, the situation will be worse. Either they'll kill me, or you'll reveal yourself while trying to protect me. I can't run anywhere. There's nowhere to hide. Besides, this Forgetting would be temporary, so how bad could it be?"

"The Forgetting would be brief, that's true, but it doesn't make it any less distasteful. Besides, making you Forget won't solve all our problems." She gestures, and a neural scan shows up. "Not by a long shot."

I stop pacing to examine the new Screen. It's my neural scan, that much is clear. My brain is a beehive of activity. It reminds me of a video I saw of an ancient city highway. Compared to the scan from yesterday, the changes are profound. Compared to two days ago, it might as well belong to a different brain.

"This is the result of you ridding me of their tampering, isn't it?" I whisper.

"Yes."

"And all these changes are after only two days without all that stuff?"

She sighs. "Now you see the problem."

"But what if you reverse this?" My throat feels like sandpaper as I say the words. Catching myself speaking out loud, I continue mentally. "What if you turn it all back on and make me like the other Youths?"

"It would take days for you to get to the point where any irregularities would be considered within the norm." Phoe makes a quick gesture and offers me the resulting cup of water. "I can't even imagine how you'd explain all this adrenaline to yourself."

"Well"—I accept the cup—"they might be searching the archives for some time, hopefully until the end of today. After that, they have the Birth Day prep and celebrations to deal with, so with any luck, they might actually only get here in a couple of days."

"We have no way of knowing if that will be enough time for you to return to the baseline of a normal Youth's neural scan," she says. "Besides, they could still decide to conduct the interrogations on Birth Day. Today is only starting, and they have until tomorrow."

"Listen, Phoe." I take a thirsty gulp from the cup. "It's *my* safety we're talking about. My plan. My mind." I gesture for the cup to dissipate. "Shouldn't it be my decision?"

Phoe steps closer to me, leans in, and says, "I'm your friend, Theo." She puts her hand on the back of my neck. "Looking out for you comes with the territory. Not to mention, it's in my nature as the ship to look out for the crew."

I feel a positive, calming energy spreading from where her hand touches my neck, though maybe it's her words that are having this effect on me. On the Screen, I see a surge of endorphins. My reaction to her small touch makes me wonder what my brain looked like when we kissed yesterday. Embarrassed by the memory and aware that she probably knows exactly what I'm thinking, I chuckle warily and say, "I'm now your crew? Does that make me the captain?"

"More like the cabin boy." She pulls her hand away and gives me a sad smile. "Seriously, though, is there any way I can dissuade you from this idea?"

"Yeah." I return her smile with as much swagger as I can muster. "Come up with a better plan."

We stand there in silence, looking at each other for a few seconds.

"Phoe." This time, I put my hand on the back of *her* neck. "They'll come for me no matter what. At least this way I'll have a good chance at staying out of trouble."

"Let's walk back," Phoe says and steps out of my reach.

She looks like she's come to a decision, but I can't tell what.

"For now, I'm just saying we should go back." As she's walking, she adds over her shoulder, "If we *are* to do this insanity, it would be better if you were in bed."

I follow her.

"Please make sure not to speak out loud anymore. I didn't give you a hard time when we were sitting by the Edge since I made sure no one was eavesdropping on us, but as we get closer to the Institute, I don't want to risk it."

"Sounds good," I think. "Do you agree with my plan?"

"Maybe." She massages her temples with her index fingers. "Yes, but I do so with great reluctance. And I hope you realize I will have to turn *everything* back on. The serotonin controls, the Oneness—all those things you hate."

"I understand."

"I will also have to turn off the Respirocytes," she says. "And I will have to do my best to copy *their* Forgetting, which means you won't be able to recall Mason, just like everyone else. Same goes for a bunch of movies and music and, most importantly, me."

"You've already said that. I get it. It's fine. It's only temporary." I step onto the pathway that leads to the Dorms. "Like you said, you'll make me remember it all afterwards."

"I will, but—" She grimaces. "Your personal identity will splinter after the Forgetting, because that part of you will cease to exist after I undo the Forgetting. Don't you get that?"

I rub my chin. "My identity?"

"Think about it. After the Forgetting, a new *you* will be formed. That Theo, the naïve Theo, will exist for a time, but afterwards, once I restore *you*—" She pauses. "I'm not sure what will happen to the naïve Theo at that point. There's simply no precedent that I'm aware of." She lets me catch up with her and puts a hand on my shoulder. "Will he, that persona, be obliterated? And if so, is that a murder of sorts? Do I have the right to do something like that? Do *you* have the right?"

"Won't it just be like remembering something I forgot?" I think pointedly while my insides inexplicably shiver. "I'm *me* no matter what I can or can't recall."

"I believe that knowing me, combined with your recent experiences—not to mention having the tampering turned off—has been a crucial turning point in your personality. Without all that, you wouldn't really be *you* anymore, and vice versa."

"But you said that the Forgetting merely blocks recall . . . that it makes us create a confabulation of the new reality," I think, my brain beginning to hurt. "That makes it sound like I'd still be me, only with a bunch of bullshit explanations as to what I can't recall."

Phoe gives me a sad look. "One can lie to oneself to the point where one becomes a different person. People have done it since antiquity."

"I'll take my chances with this identity crisis," I think with a bravado I don't truly feel. "Please don't try to talk me out of this anymore."

She doesn't respond.

We walk in silence the rest of the way to my Dorm. I guess not speaking is what it takes for Phoe to not try to talk me out of this plan. Still, it feels like a companionable silence.

"Get in bed," Phoe says after we enter my room. "It will be less disorienting for you to wake up in bed after the Forgetting. You won't have to confabulate a reason you were by the Goo so early in the morning."

My hands shake as I summon the bed.

Phoe summons the blanket for me. "It's not too late to reconsider. I haven't—"

"It's the only way." I imbue my thought with as much decisiveness as I can. "Please, do it now. The anticipation is killing me."

She nods and says softly, "Goodbye, Theo. I'll see you soon."

Her face is a pale mask as she makes the orchestra-conductor gesture.

I feel hypnotized by her delicate movements. As I watch, I feel a tsunami of drowsiness wash over me, and I don't fight it.

My eyes close, and I fall down the rabbit hole of sleep.

CHAPTER SIX

"Dude," Liam says, sounding too energetic for early morning. "Wake up."

I open my eyes, bring up a Screen, and realize the morning is not so early after all.

"Aha," Liam says. "You're up. Let's play hooky from Calculus." He kicks my bed. "To start with, anyhow."

I sit up halfway.

My mouth feels surprisingly clean, but I allow the Cleaning to happen anyway. I don't feel hungry or thirsty, which is also odd. I must've done what Liam used to do as a kid: sleep-eat in the middle of the night and deny it in the morning.

As the Cleaning progresses, I realize I feel strange. I can best describe the weird sensation as a very high level of excitement. With my heart beating frantically and my extremities cold, I feel as though I ran a marathon. Maybe it's because Birth Day is tomorrow? We finally get a day off from school, not to mention all the usual awesome extravaganzas that go along with the holiday. Am I overexcited because of that?

"Earth to Theo," Liam says, giving my bed a stronger shove. "Are we skipping Calculus or what?"

"First, I don't mind math as much as you do." I raise my hand before he can say something else. "Second, there's no way I'm risking a Quietude on Birth Day eve."

"They wouldn't," he says, but then he frowns.

"Yes, I see you remember what happened to Owen two years ago, thanks to your—"

"Hey." Liam grins. "You know he deserved it."

"Debatable," I say as I get ready for Lectures. "I'm walking to the Rock Garden. I feel too wired, so I want to do a quick meditation. Do you want to join?"

"Nah," Liam says. "But I might see you in Calculus."

"Oh?" I raise an eyebrow.

"You might be right," he says grudgingly. "Not worth the risk today. They might have another glassblowing display at the Fair tomorrow, and I don't want to miss it."

I chuckle as I walk out of the room.

On my way to the Rock Garden, I can't help but reflect on the combination of Liam and glassblowing. It's the oddest trade for him to want to take up as an Adult. Of all the different jobs and hobbies Adults have, that's not one I can imagine Liam practicing. My best guess is that it's the element of danger—literally playing with fire—that appeals to him. What makes it so hard to picture is Liam's attention deficit. If the shapes of the glass products at the Fair are anything to go by, that stuff requires patience.

"Hi, Theo." A pleasant female voice takes me out of my reverie as I pass by the statue in the Rock Garden. "Did you come here to meditate?"

I look behind the statue and see Grace getting up from a crouching position on the grass. It seems I caught her doing yoga.

"Yeah," I respond cautiously, "but I can go elsewhere."

"I'm almost finished," she says, smiling. "I haven't seen you meditate in so long. I'm glad you decided to pick it up again."

I fight my initial urge to ask if she's been spying on me. She's being civil, and I don't see a reason to be the first one to start something—especially something that could lead to a Quietude.

It's a shame how my relationship with Grace degraded over the years. She, Liam, and I were friends when we were younger, but after she got a Quietude because of our mischief, she officially stopped hanging out with us and became something of a snitch, or, as she would probably put it, an 'upstanding Oasis citizen.'

"I've had the same routine for a while and play sports after Lectures," I say when I realize she's waiting for me to answer. "So I got behind on my meditation, but today I feel really wired. With Birth Day tomorrow, I need to get centered."

"You haven't been this chatty in a long time either." Grace's smile widens. "I just have to finish three poses, so you can start setting up."

"Sure, Grace," I say, and then add without thinking, "I like seeing you smile."

Grace's smile disappears, and she gives me a confused stare.

I don't know why I said that, nor do I know why I find her big blue eyes interesting today.

"Sorry if I'm babbling," I say, blinking. "As you can see, I really need to clear my mind." I wave her on. "Go ahead, finish your yoga."

"Okay," Grace says and relaxes a little.

I look at her and wonder what possessed me to compliment her smile like some guy from an ancient movie. I'm glad she's in a good mood. Otherwise, she could've misconstrued the comment for something forbidden, and if she had, she would've told on me, since that's the way she is.

I walk over to a nice sunny spot and sit in a lotus pose.

Grace is still in my field of vision. She gets back on the ground and flawlessly executes Setu Bandhasana—the bridge pose. Liam calls it the 'bending over backwards' pose, and he's not that far off the mark. Having tried the pose myself, I know it requires an immense amount of flexibility. Grace makes it look easy.

Maybe I chose a bad spot, because I feel very hot all of a sudden.

Unable to help myself, I look back at Grace's pose. She has her pelvis high in the air, and even through her baggy Youth clothing, I can tell she has feminine curves of the kind I've seen in ancient media.

When she switches positions, I look away. But when she goes into Halasana—the plow pose—I can't help but stare at her again. I guess I'm admiring her skills. That must be it. Why else would I find this so interesting? Maybe I should try doing yoga. I know I never even tried doing the pose she's in, not after Liam compared it to trying to blow oneself. He's lucky no one but me heard him say that, or else he'd still be in Quietude.

Next, Grace gets into Adho Mukha Svanasana, also known as the 'downward-facing dog' pose. As she executes it, I wonder why this one isn't called the bridge. With her butt in the air like that, she certainly looks more like a bridge than an ancient dog.

Meditation is now the furthest thing from my mind. For some unknown reason, I can't peel my eyes from her pose. I wipe the sweat from my forehead and wonder why I find Grace's workout so hypnotizing today. Can someone get up one day and be *this* much into yoga? Also, why is my heart beating faster? Why do I feel this strange stirring in—

"It's all yours," Grace says, getting up. "Meditate away."

"Thanks," I say hoarsely.

She raises an eyebrow, so I clear my throat and add, "You've gotten very good at yoga."

"Thanks," she says and beams a megaton smile at me. "I plan to talk to the yoga masters tomorrow at the Fair. Do you think I'll impress them?"

"Oh yeah," I say, my voice somewhat more controlled. "They'll be impressed."

"Great," she says. "I'm glad I bumped into you. I needed a little encouragement."

I mumble something reassuring and close my eyes, pretending I need to get back to my meditation. Whatever jitteriness I was feeling earlier has multiplied a hundredfold.

Through my nearly closed eyelids, I spy Grace walking out of the Rock Garden with a spring in her step.

I bring up a Screen to check the time.

I have fifteen minutes to meditate, assuming I don't want to be late for Calculus.

I close my eyes and focus on my breathing.

In breath follows an out breath, over and over.

Unfortunately, instead of focusing on my breathing, my thoughts wander back to a few moments ago. What the hell was that? Why did my body react in such a strange way? I'm not even sure I understand what happened, but it does seem like something forbidden.

In. Out.

The breathing isn't helping.

I check the time. I have ten minutes left.

Getting up, I decide to try something else to clear my head.

I walk up to the nearest track and sprint as fast as I can. As my lungs start to burn, I realize how out of shape I am. My leg muscles ache as though I already ran this morning. Pushing through the discomfort, I notice the tiredness is at least providing some relief from the strange whirlwind in my mind.

As I approach the Lectures building, I decide to chalk up my earlier fascination with Grace's body to Birth Day anticipation. Regardless of what it was, I make myself a solemn promise not to discuss this with anyone, not even Liam.

I walk to Calculus by way of the male shower rooms, which are there for those of us who wish to use this method of washing instead of the waterless gesture. When I enter the shower stall, on a whim, I decide to use cold water. As the chilly liquid immerses me, I realize it was a great idea, because by the time I'm finished, I feel like I've completely gotten over the Rock Garden incident, and I'm ready to face the rest of my day.

* * *

Though I usually like the certainty of math, today I find it hard to sit still as Instructor George describes the so-called Cauchy-Riemann equations. His heart clearly isn't into his lecture today. I bet he's worried about the attendance at his booth at the Fair tomorrow, and he should be. Calculus isn't the most popular subject.

I'm equally distracted in my Debate and Philosophy Lectures, and the History Lecture reminds me of medieval torture, even though that's not the topic today. Instructor Filomena gets on her high horse to discuss the perils of technology again—her favorite topic. She talks about the carbon emissions that the technology of the ancients pumped into the air, and how the resulting greenhouse effect would've destroyed Earth if the Goo hadn't beat it to the punch. She doesn't mention the geo-engineering efforts that solved the very global warming problems she's describing, since that would ruin her argument. What really makes this session worse is that she decided to forgo my favorite part of her class, where she shows us glimpses of the ancient world.

I decide that all the Instructors must have Birth Day matters on their minds today, and thus the curriculum has suffered.

The highlight of the day is the lunch bell.

As soon as it rings, I jump to my feet and make my way into the corridor. Liam is already waiting for me.

"Want to chill in the room?" he asks. "Or should we go play something?"

"I think I want to take it easy," I say. "I ran before this, and my legs are still sore."

"All righty, then. We'll walk back like this." He walks exaggeratingly slow, like a man under water. "Or is this still too fast?"

I don't dignify his jibe with a response and walk down the corridor that leads out of the Lectures building. Once I'm outside, I turn in the direction of our Dorm, and Liam follows me.

As we walk, we debate which ancient movie we want to watch during our break. Liam takes advantage of my distracted state by choosing a cartoon I've never heard of. It's called *Kung Fu Panda.*

"If it sucks, which it will, can we watch something else?" I say as we enter the building.

"Yeah," he says. "If we *agree* that it sucks, then sure."

We discuss everything we know about pandas, which isn't much, since they're one of the few creatures that are missing from the Zoo.

"Yuck. Do you smell that?" I say as we approach our room's door. "Did you fart?"

There's very rarely, if ever, foul smells in Oasis. Food bars don't usually make anyone gassy, but we do know the sensation, since it happens after eating non-regular food at the Birth Day celebrations. Also, on rare occasions, our bowel movements have a farting prelude, much to Liam's delight.

"It wasn't me," he says, confused.

I wrinkle my nose as I take a couple of steps.

"Dude, watch out," Liam says, pointing down.

I jump back, fully expecting to see a spider or some other horrible critter from the Zoo.

What I actually see is worse in a way.

It's a pile of excrement.

"Crap," I say.

"Literally," Liam says.

"I almost stepped in it," I say. "Where did it come from?"

"It's Owen," Liam says through his teeth. "But this is really low and disgusting, even for him."

"What do we do?" I sweep my hand over the pile, and it evaporates. "We need to retaliate, but it needs to be something low-key. We don't want to jeopardize Birth Day."

"I have an idea," Liam says. "Follow me."

He determinedly walks through the corridors to where Owen and his posse share their lodgings. When he reaches their door, he crosses his fingers and whispers, "Let's hope they aren't there." Out loud, he yells, "Owen, this is Liam and Theo. We want to organize a study group. Are you in there?"

When no one responds, Liam gives me a devilish grin and executes the door-opening gesture.

The door obeys.

No one seems to be inside, so we gingerly walk in.

"Jackpot," Liam says after we verify that the room is empty. "Help me with this." Liam makes the palm-up gesture, and a bar of Food appears in his hand. He drops the bar on the floor and repeats the motion. Another bar of Food appears on his palm, and he drops it on the floor too, next to the first piece.

I catch on and make a Food bar appear, then drop it on the floor. Then I do it over and over again.

It takes us almost the whole break to fill up most of Owen's room with Food bars. Then, laughing, we head back to Lectures. I can't even imagine what Owen's expression will be when he opens his door to find his room completely flooded with bars of Food.

The rest of the school day is easier to get through. My hand got tired from the Food prank, but paradoxically, the activity also soothed my mind. When the lessons get particularly boring, all I have to do is picture Owen entering his room, very tired, and a smile shows up on my face. He'll be cursing and making sweeping gestures similar to the one I used to get rid of his prank, but each gesture will only get rid of a single Food bar at a time. Liam and I verified that by doing a test. Owen will be beyond pissed at having to perform all those cleaning gestures.

A final bell rings, and I yawn as I get up.

"Let's play soccer," Liam says when we exit the Lectures Hall, "or basketball."

"Why don't you do that without me," I say. "I'm tired, and I want to get some sleep. I'd rather save my energy for Birth Day."

"Suit yourself," Liam says. He feigns nonchalance, a sign that he's actually disappointed.

"Sorry, dude." I yawn again. "I'm just feeling tired for some reason."

"Just go," he says, suppressing a yawn of his own. "Go before you infect me with your yawning."

He talks to me as we walk in the direction of the Dorm, and I give him sleepy, monosyllabic responses until he takes off for the soccer field.

I walk the rest of the way on my own, glad for the silence.

When I get into bed, I experience Oneness, which is extremely intense today. The pleasure in the beginning is almost painful. As I adjust to it, I feel the presence. Oddly, an unbidden vision of a surreal, pixie-haired goddess enters my consciousness. The presence is usually vague, just an ethereal sensation without a specific focal point. I don't worry about the visage, though. I've heard of Youths describing this part of Oneness as speaking with angels or the gods of the ancients, though we all know that's just an illusion.

The next step of Oneness is the unsolicited feeling of love and kindness toward everything and everyone, but I don't get a chance to experience it as I fall deeply into sleep.

CHAPTER SEVEN

I'm running along the Great Wall of China. A moment later, I'm gazing up at the Empire State Building.

"Theo," someone says, and I realize I was dreaming of pre-Goo times.

Reluctant to let go of the dream, I pretend I'm still sleeping.

"Dude." The voice is louder. "You're sleeping through Birth Day."

I instantly open my eyes.

"You sleep too much," Liam says, splashing some water from his cup onto my face. "Especially for someone who went to bed as early as you did."

Wiping the water off my face, I look him over. Liam is dressed in a special Birth Day edition of clothes. They look more like an ancient outfit than our usual shapeless gray jumpsuit/scrubs. Everyone's wearing clothes of varying colors and designs today. In Liam's case, he's dressed in green overalls, similar to what farmers used to wear.

"I had a cool dream," I say. My voice is groggy from sleep, so I clear my throat. "I dreamed of places from pre-Armageddon times. There was no Goo, and I could walk or run in any direction for as long as I wanted."

Liam waves at me dismissively and says, "Sounds like the beginning of Filomena's class."

I grimace. "No talk of Lectures today. We don't get days off often enough for that."

"Good thinking," Liam says and extends his hand for a bar of Food.

I sit up in bed. "Dude, leave room for the ancient food they'll have at the Fair."

He stuffs his mouth with the Food bar and mumbles something that sounds like, "I don't like that stuff." He chews a little bit and adds, "It smells funny, and it's hot to the touch."

"That's the point," I say and get up. "It's how food was, back in the day when it was 'cooked.'"

I look down at my outfit. Unlike Liam's green clothing, my clothes are predominately blue, reminding me of jeans. I'm also wearing a blue sleeveless t-shirt, which is a huge improvement over our usual clothing.

Liam uses my distraction to chew more of his Food and then says, "Still sounds like history. Maybe you should swing by Filomena's booth."

"Sure." I roll my eyes. "Right after I stand on my head for a few hours."

Liam grins. "I can stand on my head for twenty minutes."

I don't say anything; if I challenge his statement, he'll actually do it to prove that he can. In many ways, Liam is the most immature Youth out of the batch of us turning twenty-four today. So instead of buying into his craziness, I say, "Ready to go?"

Without waiting for his reply, I hurry to the door. Then, without looking back, I make my way outside.

Okay, so maybe Liam's immaturity has rubbed off on me.

When I exit, I see that everything is already set up.

I can hear at least two genres of music—classical and electronic. Large, colorful floats hang high in the air, right under the Dome, and brightly dressed Youths are walking around. The Institute grounds are covered with Birth Day paraphernalia, including a dance platform and food stalls. In the distance, the Adults have set up their career and hobby exhibitions, as usual.

"Are the glassblowers there?" Liam asks. His eyes are pinholes as he scans the distant region of the Fair.

"I don't know," I say. "I'm starving, so I'm starting my explorations with the food stalls."

"See you later then," Liam says and sprints away.

I walk leisurely, allowing my nose to carry me toward the smell of fried dough, which is one of the highlights of Birth Day. The Adults have recreated other ancient foods, such as French fries, pretzels, and popcorn, but fried dough is still my favorite to this day.

I wonder if there'll be something new to taste this year. The Adults get pretty creative; in fact, they have a whole field of study called Culinary Anthropology. After they give you the treat, they tell you about it in the same way other Adults talk about their passions. Last year, the Culinary folks told me they recreate anything they possibly can, so long as it doesn't require something like the meat of animals or other things that no longer exist. And sometimes, they don't let the lack of authenticity stop them. One year, they tried to make some kind of fake hotdog, which became a Birth Day legend because of how atrocious it tasted. Or maybe everyone was grossed out by the idea of eating a cooked dog, even a fake one. Those animals are so cute at the Zoo.

In general, I don't know what the ancients were thinking when they decided to eat the flesh of living creatures. Then again, they did crazier things than that 'for fun,' like inhaling cancer-causing chemicals or diving into oceans with just a barrel of oxygen on their backs. Perhaps insanity was part of being mortal. With their relatively short lifespans, the ancients didn't value their lives or the lives of other people and creatures as much as we, their immortal descendants, do.

I inhale the smell of fried dough again. Okay, I'll be first to admit that even when it's drowned in powdered sugar, this treat *isn't* tastier than Food. Liam was right in that the two aren't comparable, especially considering that this stuff is loaded with things that are really bad for one's health. Even eating them once a year has to be limited to one or two pieces, max. I found the wisdom in that limit the hard way, when I ate four pieces (two of mine and two of Liam's). I felt so sick I had to go to the nurse's office. All that aside, it's something different, which I like. Plus, it's a traditional food the ancients ate at carnivals and fairs, so I'm following a tried-and-true tradition.

As I pass the dance floor, I see Youths of all ages dancing to upbeat music that gives my step a little bounce.

With all this merriment, it's almost possible to forget that we're the last remnants of humanity, surrounded by deadly Goo on all sides—which may be one of the purposes of Birth Day.

When I get to the food stalls, I see Youths already lined up, and I silently curse myself. I should've set an alarm to wake up earlier today.

The largest cluster of people is by the fried dough, proving that other people also find it the best treat of the bunch. I stand behind an older-looking guy and wonder if he'll be leaving the ranks of Youths today to become an Adult. Then I wonder if Adults celebrate Birth Day the same way we do. If not, this might be this guy's last chance to eat fried dough.

To kill time, I bring up my Screen.

The Adults sent out a color-coded map of the Institute and a list of activities we can find here today. Bursting with excitement, I inspect the different hobby and career options, making a mental note to check out the painters, sculptors, and every one of the professional athletes' stalls.

Like in the prior years, there'll be championship games in a variety of active sports and some more brainy activities, such as chess. This should be fun, as long as we don't compete with the Adults who chose those occupations. Last year, Liam and I played on a team of eleven Youths against three Adults who've made soccer their lifelong study. Our numbers didn't help. The three Adults handed our asses to us in a defeat so crushing I'm too embarrassed to mention the final score.

The fried dough line crawls forward. The smell is getting stronger, making my mouth water.

To keep sane, I look at the Screen again. There's a mention of secret prizes, plus a forest egg hunt, which is a new activity and something I think Liam will be willing to check out with me. When it gets darker, the day will end with the traditional aurora borealis display that will culminate in fireworks.

"Theodore," a raspy voice says from behind me. "I need you to come with me."

The Youths in front of me, including the nearly Adult-aged guy, look scared.

Reluctantly, I turn around.

All it takes is a glance at the dreaded visor to recognize the source of their fear.

It's a Guard.

My adrenaline spikes. What does he want with me? I've been careful not to get into trouble.

"What's going on?" I ask the Guard. "Did I do something wrong?"

"Please follow me," the Guard says with a steel edge to his voice. "Make haste."

"Can I at least grab a fried d—"

The Guard moves his hand in a strange motion.

I'm hit with an intense sense of relaxation.

My hands drop to my sides.

It's actually rather nice and timely that I got a chance to calm down. Resisting a Guard's commands can double or triple your Quietude—something I learned a long time ago.

"Follow me?" the Guard half-asks, half-commands.

I nod and exit the line.

The Guard turns and heads away from the food stalls. I walk to his right so he can see me. I know the drill.

As we pass by all the merriment, I curse my horrible fate. I'm tempted to ask the Guard what the problem is, but I know that might result in a longer Quietude.

What's really odd is that we're not walking toward the Quietude building. We're heading southeast, in the opposite direction.

I glimpse another Guard. This one has a female Youth walking next to him. She's wearing a long Birth Day summer dress that's somewhere between pink and magenta in hue. Spotting her red hair, I realize it's Grace, except that makes no sense. Why would *she* be in trouble? Did Miss Good Behavior finally manage to misbehave?

Grace sees me and raises an eyebrow but keeps walking, the epitome of obedience.

As we walk, an idea enters my now-paranoid mind. Is Grace here to give testimony? Is this reckoning related to my staring at her yesterday? Did she notice me watching her do those yoga poses? She didn't seem aware of me when she was exercising, and she couldn't have known what I was thinking, even if she had seen me looking. Even I don't fully understand what came over me that morning. All I know is that it was something forbidden. Still, given Grace's presence, I have to consider the unpleasant possibility that this walk is related to that incident. I imagine Adults asking me questions about that incident, and my cheeks burn.

Farther away, another Guard and another person are walking in our direction. As they approach, I recognize the Youth-hyena hybrid accompanying the Guard.

It's Owen.

This pair makes more sense. Like Liam and me, Owen is no stranger to Quietudes or trouble in general. Could *he* be the reason we're here? Did he tell the Adults about Liam and me filling his room with Food bars last night? That doesn't seem like Owen. Though he's a bully and a jackass, Owen has a code, of sorts. He's never once ratted us out, and we've returned the favor. Why change that pattern now, over such a minor prank? If it came down to it, if we told the Adults about the literal shit he gave us last night, he'd be in a lot more trouble than Liam or me. Plus, how does Grace fit into everything?

This is getting really odd.

On the bright side, I think I know where they're taking us. We're all heading straight for the cube that is the Administrative building. I've been to that place a few times before, but I'm guessing Grace is very familiar with it. The building is where one goes to rat on someone, which I never have. In my case, I was brought there to hear a lecture from the Dean on the subject of 'being a good citizen of Oasis'—something reserved for the severest troublemakers.

I can't help but ask the Guard, "Why are we going to the Administrative building?"

The Guard doesn't reply; he just does something with his hand.

I feel relaxed again and realize that maybe things aren't so bad. Maybe the three of us need to help the Adults with something that has nothing to do with us being in trouble.

My Guard and I are the first to enter the building, and he leads me through the empty corridors towards the Dean's office. Only now do I realize that the Dean, along with all the other Adults, is probably too busy with Birth Day to deal with us.

My suspicion is confirmed when we enter the waiting area. Usually there's a receptionist here. Today, there's only one person waiting for us.

Liam.

My usually hyperactive friend looks pretty calm, all things considered. I suspect he's playing it cool in front of the Guard.

"Someone will be with you shortly," the Guard says. "Don't go anywhere."

He gestures to lock the door leading out of the waiting room. When Adults do that, any Youth who tries the door-opening gesture doesn't get results. However, unlike a Quietude, confinement in a room is no big deal. It can even be seen as a vacation from Lectures, since Screens and everything else work the way they usually do. The nurse does this when Liam or I pretend to be sick. I say 'pretend' because only a few of my visits to the nurse's office have been for real. I bet the same goes for Liam. I don't know about him, but I can count on my fingers the number of times I've been genuinely sick.

"Dude," Liam whispers as soon as the door closes behind the Guard. "Why are we here?"

"I don't know—" I begin to say, but the door opens again, and the two other Guards bring in Grace and Owen.

"Thank you, Albert," says the shorter, smaller-framed Guard in a strangely textured female voice. "We'll summon you if you're needed."

The taller Guard, Albert, nods and leaves the room.

As the door closes, Liam and I exchange glances. Two things are unusual about that little exchange:

First, we've only come across a female Guard once, during an incident with a fallen tree. Second, Guards *never* call each other by their first names in front of us.

Judging by the canine alertness on Owen's face, he also noticed at least one of these irregularities.

"Please sit," the female Guard says to Owen and Grace. "Theodore, be prepared to talk to us in a minute." She makes the door-locking gesture and says, "Let me just set things up."

She heads into the Dean's office.

As soon as the door closes behind the Guard, Owen jumps to his feet and looks at me. "Why-Odor?"

I don't say anything, but I'm gripped by sudden anger—anger more potent than anything I've experienced since childhood. Did Owen's stupid nickname cause it?

Oblivious to my emotional state, Owen gives Liam a onceover and says, "Li-Li-Kins? Did one of you stoop to ratting? Is that why your little girlfriend is here?" He glares at Grace before saying to Liam, "Did you decide to take lessons from the biggest snitch in the Institute?"

Grace looks like he slapped her. Her eyes glint with moisture.

Surprisingly, I feel bad for her. She must be so overwhelmed over getting into trouble with us. Also, seeing her upset makes me angrier, even if what Owen said isn't exactly undeserved. I guess I just don't like seeing anyone get bullied. I suppress my emotions, reminding myself that we're a shout away from the Guards.

"How was your dinner, Slowen?" Liam asks, using a nickname for Owen that never caught on.

"You mean the stuff you left me?" Owen replies without hesitation. "It wasn't so bad, compared to yours. Speaking of which, did you eat everything I left you, Theo, or did you guys have to split it?"

Without fully understanding what I'm doing, I get up.

Owen gives me an uncaring look and says, "Do you want to dance with me? You should wait till all this is over—"

"If you don't shut the fuck up, your new nickname will be Swollen," I say, my teeth grinding painfully in my effort to rein in my anger.

Liam gets up and stands behind me.

Grace gives me a horrified look.

Belatedly, I realize I said the F-word in front of her. My Quietude is a guarantee now, even if the Guards brought us here on benign business.

Owen looks ecstatic, as he also understands this fact.

Seething, I ball my hands into fists. He provoked me on purpose, on Birth Day of all days. Maybe I was wrong about him possessing a code.

The anticipation of losing all that Birth Day fun feeds my fury, and I step toward Owen. If I'm going to miss out on Birth Day anyway, I might as well get satisfaction of a different kind.

There's a glimmer of fear in Owen's eyes.

I feel a hand on my shoulder, and Liam says, "Dude, what the hell are you doing?"

I exhale.

He's right.

Was I about to hit Owen?

What the hell is going on with me?

The door opens.

A helmeted head peeks out, and a female voice says, "Theo, please join us."

CHAPTER EIGHT

I unclench my fists before the female Guard can see them. Taking a calming breath, I walk toward the door.

I can't help but notice she's the first Guard, and a rare Adult, to call me 'Theo' instead of 'Theodore.' Another oddity, albeit a smaller one.

"Sit there," says the male Guard, nodding toward one of the Dean's guest chairs.

He takes the Dean's chair and the female Guard sits to the side, on another guest chair.

This little exchange sets a record for the longest conversation I've ever had with a Guard. Of course, I don't mention that, knowing full well that speaking will likely get me into more trouble.

"I need you to do as I tell you," says the male Guard, his voice icy. "If you do, you'll be out of here quickly."

"Please," the female Guard adds in a softer tone. "I can imagine how much you want to get back to Birth Day."

It might be my imagination, but did she turn her helmet toward her colleague in a show of disapproval? Why would she do that? Are they playing 'good cop, bad cop,' like in the ancient movies?

"I'll do as you tell me," I say as evenly as I can. Then, with a little bitterness, I add, "It's not like I have a choice."

"Good," says the male Guard. "Put your hand to your chest."

"Huh?" I look into his mirrored helmet, but all I see is the spherically distorted reflection of my own puzzled face.

"Like this," the female guard says, placing her arm across her chest.

"Stop stalling," the male voice says sternly.

I cautiously raise my hand to my chest, and the female Guard nods in approval.

"Say, 'I consent to the Lens of Truth and swear to tell the truth and nothing but the truth,'" the male Guard says.

"What?" I look from one Guard to the other.

The male Guard drums his fingers on the desk. "Do you *want* a Quietude?"

I vigorously shake my head.

"Then say, 'I consent to the Lens of Truth.'"

"I consent to the Lens of Truth," I say, but in a small act of defiance, I do my best to sound as unenthusiastic as I can.

"And swear to tell the truth and nothing but the truth," he prompts.

"And swear to tell the truth and nothing but the truth," I repeat robotically.

A peculiar sensation washes over me. It feels as though a phase of Oneness suddenly emerged inside my consciousness, except I feel incorporeal. During Oneness, I feel connected to imaginary, faraway galaxies and stars, but now, it's as if I'm no longer inhabiting my body . . . as if I'm some kind of ancient spirit.

"State your name," comes a voice.

From where I'm 'floating,' I can't tell which Guard asked me the question. Then suddenly, back in my body, my mouth moves without my volition. It says, "Theodore."

From my perch outside my body, I find it more than odd that my mouth can speak without me willing it. And why did it use such a formal version of my name?

"How old are you, Theodore?" a voice asks.

"I turned twenty-four today," I say again without meaning to.

"Ask him something he would *want* to lie about," a voice says. "Let's make sure the compulsion really works."

"Okay," says what I have to assume is the other voice. "Bring up his neural scan."

My mouth stays shut this time. They didn't ask me a question.

"Have you done anything inappropriate today, Theodore?" a voice asks. "If not today, then how about yesterday?"

"I felt inappropriate sensations as I watched Grace do yoga," my mouth says. I'm appalled. I want to jump back into my body and stop my stupid mouth from saying these things, but I can't get back, no matter how much I yearn for control. As though to spite me, my mouth continues. "Additionally, I played a prank on Owen. We filled his room with Food bars." *No*, I mentally scream at my mouth, but I can feel it isn't done yet. Despite my titanic effort to silence it, my mouth opens and utters, "Finally, I used the F-word a few minutes ago."

At least my mouth didn't reveal that I nearly attacked Owen. I guess it doesn't consider 'nearly doing something' as 'actually doing something.'

The voices confer in hushed tones. All I hear is, "His neural activity is extremely bizarre, but the Lens is clearly working."

"What happened to Mason, Theodore?" a voice asks. "Do you know who Mason is?"

"I don't understand those two questions," my mouth says. "Are you talking about the people who worked with stones? People from History Lecture? Or do you mean the secret society?"

"Did you make the Council Forget a meeting?" a voice asks.

"I don't understand this question either," my mouth says. "What council? What meeting?"

"Why is your neural scan so erratic?" a voice asks.

"I don't know," my mouth replies.

For what feels like an hour, the voice asks more of these meaningless questions. My mouth pretty much always answers, 'No,' interspersed with the occasional, 'I don't know.'

"Do you understand what has happened?" a voice finally asks.

"No," my mouth says.

My consciousness rushes back into my body, and I instantly feel in control of my mouth and other faculties, except it's too late. I already told them about the yoga incident and the prank, not to mention my use of vulgarity.

I'm screwed.

I look from one Guard to the other. Given their reflective helmets, it's impossible to tell how upset or disappointed they are.

I look to the side.

There's a large Screen with neural activity on display.

Given one of the questions I was asked, it doesn't take a big leap to figure out that it's my scan we're looking at.

Examining my brain scans has been a sort of hobby of mine over the years. What I see here looks nothing like the scans I've seen before. The image sends a chill down my spine. Is all this abnormal activity a side effect of something they did to me?

The female Guard gets up, distracting me from my thoughts.

"Follow me," she says, her voice oddly comforting.

She heads for the door, and I get up and follow, my feet dragging as though my shoes are filled with lead.

When I enter the waiting room, Liam, Grace, and Owen look at me questioningly. I give them a shrug and make my face into as confused an expression as I can. I don't know what to tell them. Nothing that happened inside the Dean's office makes sense. Of course, even if I had anything to say, it wouldn't be safe to say it in front of the Guard.

The female Guard passes through the room, gestures for the door to open, and makes sure I exit ahead of her. She then joins me in the corridor and meticulously gestures to lock the door behind us, as though Liam and the others are crazy enough to run away under these circumstances.

Leading me down the long corridor, she brings me to a room I've never seen. Judging by its lofty size and a couple of comfortable couches in the middle, this is some kind of administrative lounge area.

"Stay here," the female Guard says. "Once we're done questioning the others, you can go back to the festivities. It shouldn't take longer than an hour."

As soon as she closes the door behind her, I begin to pace.

Nothing makes sense.

Why did she say I'd be going back to the festivities? I confessed to enough wrongdoings to be in Quietude for a long time. Why would they let that slide?

These thoughts bring me back to a deeper mystery: Why *did* I answer those questions without wanting to? And what was the purpose of those questions?

On a whim, as I circle the room, I make a door-opening gesture. I'm certain the Guard locked the door behind her, but it's not like I have anything else to do.

To my shock, the door opens.

I step across the threshold, but the strangest thing happens.

Part of me—at least I think that's what it is—says in a voice that's not my own, "Don't leave, Theo."

This voice in my head is extremely weird for several reasons, not the least of which is that it sounds feminine.

"Sit on the couch," the voice says. "You might feel disoriented as I restore your memory."

I have no idea who the voice belongs to or what it's trying to tell me, but sitting sounds like the best idea I've had in a long time. I walk over to a couch and sit down.

Out of the corner of my eye, I see the door close.

A strange avalanche of sensations floods my head. I feel a horrible sense of vertigo and a sudden need to lie down.

As soon as my head touches the cushion, drowsiness overwhelms me.

I close my eyes, and my awareness goes away.

CHAPTER NINE

I open my eyes.

Did I just wake up?

Looking around the room, I find it too large to be the one Liam and I share.

Then it hits me: this is the Administrative building.

I remember what happened.

I remember *everything* that happened.

I also realize I'm no longer alone in the room.

A familiar pixie-haired woman is sitting next to me on the couch.

"Phoe," I exclaim, sitting up. "I'm back."

"Don't talk out loud," she says and gives me a worried smile.

I examine my memories.

As far as I can tell, they're all back. Then again, I didn't think I was missing any information a minute ago, when I was missing *everything.*

I recall Phoe and everything that happened from the very first day she spoke to me. I remember Mason from when we were little kids to his demise. I also recall, in detail, what it felt like to *not* remember these things. It's like that 'on the tip of your tongue' sensation. After you *do* recall the trivial detail that eluded your brain, you can't believe you blanked on something so basic. Except in my case, this happened with hordes of important facts.

I also realize how much easier my life was when I didn't remember these things. How much happier I was in my ignorance.

Phoe's fears about my split identity weren't exactly valid. Yes, a more innocent Theo existed for a time, but he isn't dead. He's part of me, the Theo who's more complete but wishes he wasn't. I internalize everything he experienced the way I imagine drunk ancients internalized all the crazy things they did while intoxicated.

"This really isn't a good time to philosophize about the question of identity," Phoe says in an urgent whisper and moves closer to me. "We need to talk, right after I do this."

Before I understand what's happening, her lips are on mine.

I return the kiss. Somehow, the physical closeness clears the remaining grogginess from my mind. I remember doing this with her, the day before yesterday. Only it feels different right now. More primal.

The kiss continues, and she moves closer to me on the couch. She's so close that her soft chest brushes against my upper arm.

I feel a stirring.

It's familiar.

It's what happened yesterday when I was watching Grace, only this sensation is many times stronger.

Phoe pulls away, her eyes narrowed into slits.

"I still can't believe *that* happened." She crosses her arms in front of her chest. "I can't believe you were lusting after Grace."

"Phoe," I think and stare into her eyes. "Are you actually jealous? You know I didn't remember—"

"Bah." Her lips twist. "Why should I be? After all, I'm literally a heartless AI. Why would you think it's wrong to be attracted to someone else?"

"Phoe, I wasn't myself." I put my hand on hers, feeling the warmth of her skin. "More importantly, I don't *want* Grace." I think this with emphasis, doing my best not to blush at the extreme taboo of this topic. "If I did . . ." I inhale, unsure how to proceed. "If I decided to want anyone *in that way*, there's no doubt in my mind it would be *you*." As I subvocalize it, it occurs to me that this is how I really feel and that I was hiding this truth from myself.

Phoe looks uncertain, so I squeeze her hand and say mentally, "If you need my permission to scan my mind to prove I'm telling you the truth, go ahead."

She gives me an unreadable look. Then, as suddenly as before, she kisses me, almost as though trying to catch me off-guard.

Not missing a beat, I kiss her back.

As we explore each other's mouths, the kiss becomes an outlet for something else. Nervousness and tension leave my body, and a meditation-like trance comes over me as I focus on the way her lips affect me. My breathing becomes shallow, and I put my hand on her lower back, feeling the delicate curve of her spine.

"Look, Theo," Phoe says, reluctantly pulling away. "I know I started this, but we really ought to stop. If they watch the recording of this room, they might wonder why you're moving your lips and tongue like a crazy person. It's an especially bad idea given that the neural scan they saw was a hot mess."

Her words work as effectively as a cold shower.

"Did you open the door for me a moment ago?" I subvocalize, changing the subject. "And if so, why did you stop me from leaving?"

"No, I didn't open that door." She gives me a wide grin. "That was all you."

"Me?" I subvocalize so loudly it almost comes out as a whisper. "But how? Did the female Guard—who must be Fiona—not lock it?"

"Yes, it is Fiona, and yes, she locked it all right. You just opened it anyway."

"How? Only Adults can undo those types of locks."

Phoe's eyes are glowing. "And the Elderly."

"Right," I think. "What does that have to do with me?" A flash of insight hits me. "Wait a minute. Are you saying what I think you're saying?"

"When Birth Day started, I modified your age, like I told you I would." She's as excited as Liam after a prank. "As far as the back end of all the security systems in Oasis is concerned, you're now ninety years old."

I stare at her blankly. The implications are too far-reaching.

"I can open any door the Adults can?"

"Yes, and many, many more." Phoe's feet drum on the floor. "For example, the Adults can't cross the boundary into the Elderly territory, but you can. You can pretty much go anywhere you want, as long as we overcome the minor problem of your youthful looks."

"Yeah." I chuckle nervously. "*That* itsy-bitsy problem."

"I have an idea about that—a plan of sorts," Phoe says. "If it works, you'll be able to travel across Oasis without any issues. But before we talk about that, I have to show you something else, something way more urgent." She looks distant for a fraction of a second. "Crap, they're coming. We should continue this *after* they lead you out of here."

"Lead me out?" I think and look at her with barely concealed hope. "Are they letting me go?"

Phoe looks at the door instead of answering.

The door opens.

A Guard is standing there.

"Theodore," he says.

I get up.

I think this is Jeremiah, though his voice is hard to recognize through the helmet's distortion. I can tell this isn't Fiona, because the voice isn't female and he's taller than her.

"Follow me," maybe-Jeremiah says and waves at me.

"He tried to soothe you again," Phoe whispers as a voice in my head.

"I wish it worked," I think, feeling my heart racing as I'm forced to walk swiftly to keep up with probably-Jeremiah's angry gait.

"Looks like they won't give me a Quietude despite all those things my mouth blabbed on about while I was under the Lens's compulsion," I think at Phoe.

"No," Phoe replies. "They probably don't care about such trivialities today. They're focused on the investigation for the Envoy—the investigation I might 'aid' very soon. Also, they'll likely make you Forget you ever saw them, which would make a Quietude odd, since you wouldn't recall how you got into trouble."

"Go," the Guard says when we reach the outdoors. He waves toward the Birth Day celebrations in the distance. "Stay out of trouble."

I immediately walk away, not needing to be told *this* twice.

Maybe-Jeremiah goes back into the building, presumably to get the others.

"Just as I thought," Phoe says. "He tried to make you Forget everything that happened. Go somewhere private and do it quickly, unless you want to run into Liam, Grace, or Owen."

I head for the nearest structure, which happens to be the cuboid Lectures building. Seeing it deserted might be interesting. This idea never came to me on prior Birth Days because there's always too much other fun stuff to do.

Phoe is silent until I enter the building, walk into a Lectures Hall, and sit.

"Okay," she says and brings up one of the giant Screens that Instructors sometimes use to put their notes on. "This is that urgent bit of information I mentioned earlier. Just don't panic."

I bet the words 'don't panic' are among the most ominous phrases ever uttered, on par with 'oh no' and 'this will only hurt a bit.'

On the Screen, I see the Dean's room, only it's just Jeremiah and Fiona there now.

"He's just a Youth," Fiona says forcefully. "Despite all the technology in the world, they sometimes have hormonal imbalances. You know what those things can do. Isn't it why they're kept separate? As a Youth, I once got my period despite all the preventative measures. My neural scan prior to that was—"

"Stop." Jeremiah's white-gloved hand covers his helmeted head as though he's dodging a thrown object. "Are you trying to make me vomit?"

"It's just biology," Fiona says, but Jeremiah raises his hand, palm out, to stop her from speaking.

"I'm not aware of any natural reason his neural scan would look like *that*," he says, lowering his hand. "He's a male, so your disgusting little story doesn't apply. However, I *have* seen scans of Youths and Adults who were deemed insane, and though his is slightly different from those, it's similar enough that I still insist he be Forgotten, for the good of our society. He's not violent yet, but that is where this usually leads."

"Fine. We'll talk to the Council, and together, we'll decide." She cracks her knuckles.

"I don't see the point in wasting our time with bureaucracy. We have an investigation to conduct and—"

"Have you ever Forgetten someone without formally clearing it with the Council?" Fiona places her hands sharply on her hips. "Because you asking me this makes me wonder—"

"Of course not," Jeremiah says, a little too quickly and defensively.

"Then I don't understand the necessity of bypassing proper protocols this time either," she says, her tone cold and formal.

"Like I said, the reason should be obvious, and time is of the essence," Jeremiah says. "We learned nothing in regards to our ultimate goal, and instead of needless Council deliberation, as two senior members, surely we can—"

"My vote would be against Forgetting him," Fiona says, raising her chin. "I will say so at the Council meeting, should we have one. If you want to save time, we can easily agree to dismiss this matter, as we don't need the Council for that. Otherwise, the whole Council will have to weigh in."

"Fine." Jeremiah's posture is tense. "Theodore can wait. Let's gather the Instructors and Mason's more distant acquaintances."

"Sounds good." Fiona squares her shoulders. "I'll get Filomena and George to start. Meanwhile, you let the children go. They've missed enough of the festivities because of your impatience, and until and unless we bring his neural scan to the attention of the Council, 'they' also includes Theo."

Jeremiah storms out of the room without saying another word.

The Screen goes blank.

"Shit," I whisper to Phoe. "Do you think they'll take it to the Council? And if they do, how do you think they'll vote?"

"I don't know," Phoe says. "Which is why getting me more resources is a matter of priority. With more resources, I should be able to figure out a way to manipulate the Elderly without risking exposure to the Envoy."

I recall her talking about an idea she had, something to do with a very dubious-sounding Test the Adults take before they become the Elderly. Only then, her excuse for having me take the Test was to help her figure out where we are in the cosmos.

"I'm not denying that knowing our current location in space and time is an important task," Phoe says, pursing her lips. "But I'm insulted if you're insinuating your wellbeing is less important to me in any way."

I realize I hinted at something like that, which is unfair to Phoe. She has literally been a lifesaver. Also, even if she is being a little self-serving when it comes to regaining her mental capacity, how can I blame her, especially after I just experienced Forgetting so intimately? Unsure how to verbalize any of this, I change the subject. "You said you could 'aid' in their investigation," I say. "Can you tell me about *that?*"

"Ah." She gives me an impish grin. "Remember that Keeper archive?"

"Yes."

"When Jeremiah showed it to Fiona, he also, without meaning to, led me right to it." She summons a chair and sits down. "Now I can plant this little pearl in there for him to find."

The Screen comes to life with a grainy image of a Council meeting.

"Ladies and Gentlemen of the Council," Fiona says in the recording. "Despite your vote, I urge you to reconsider." Her eyes look sad. "You know I was against Theodore's Forgetting." She gives Jeremiah a seething look. "But this new turn of events—the *torture* of a Youth—"

"Questioning," Jeremiah corrects. "Persuasive questioning."

"Torture," Fiona insists. "I find the very idea abhorrent. Why don't you talk to the Envoy? There are other options when it comes to obtaining information. Perhaps the Lens of—"

"I will not bother the Envoy with this matter," Jeremiah says, his eyes beaming wrath. "He would want me to present him with answers and results, not problems for *him* to solve. You choose to ignore the fact that this Youth has resisted Punish, Forgetting, and a slew of other technologies. Why would the Lens of Truth be any different?"

"Because—"

Phoe waves her hand to pause the video, stopping Fiona mid-argument.

"Don't worry," Phoe says. "What you just saw is not *it*. Quite the opposite. I will delete this part of the recording so thoroughly, even *I* won't be able to find an echo of it ever again. I kept it to show *you*, so you'll understand the context of what's about to follow in the portion of the video I plan to use."

"This recording is from two days ago, right?" I subvocalize. "It's from that meeting you made them Forget?"

"Yes, it's from that meeting," Phoe says. "Fiona really was against them torturing you, as you saw. I recorded this because I wanted to know how they voted. Plus, I had some free time while you were in the IRES game. And now, my recording is about to pay big dividends."

With a motion, she fast-forwards the video.

"This," she says. "This is what I'll cut out and stick in the archive."

She resumes the video.

Fiona storms toward the exit, but before she reaches it, she turns around, gives every Council member a baleful glare, and says, "As of now, I formally resign as a member of this ruling body."

The room comes alive with hushed murmurs and outraged whispers.

To Jeremiah, Fiona says, "Once I'm officially off the Council, I wish to Forget this latest decision . . . and I hope it eats a hole through the amorphous pit you call your conscience."

Not waiting for anyone's response, Fiona storms out of the room.

Phoe makes the Screen go blank again.

"Wow," I subvocalize. "She quit the Council *and* told them off."

"Yep. If I hadn't made them Forget, it would've happened that way, but as is, they don't remember her outburst. Once he sees this, Jeremiah might strongly suspect Fiona to be the person he's looking for," Phoe says triumphantly. "She has a strong motive. She basically told them she hates their guts. On top of that, she even said something about Forgetting."

"Can't she accuse him of faking this video?" I think.

"She could, but it would be reasonable for him to state that he doesn't have the resources or capabilities to create something like that," Phoe says, then gives me a thoughtful look. "I have to say, faking a video is a very interesting idea. It wouldn't be much harder than manipulating Augmented Reality—"

"Okay," I think in an effort to keep Phoe focused. "Even if everyone thought this video was real, I don't see how it would help us."

"Are you nuts? If Jeremiah has a suspect, he'll stop looking for you. That aside, it's the oldest trick in the world." Phoe tilts her head. "We're dividing and conquering them. While Fiona and Jeremiah fight each other, we'll do what we need to do: the Test. The likeliest outcome of their fight will be Jeremiah reporting Fiona to the Envoy. From there, they'll question Fiona with the Lens of Truth. The questioning will prove her to be innocent, except they might think she made herself Forget. Things will get complicated for them, which is great for us. Maybe Jeremiah will talk the Envoy into letting him question more Council members. He's clearly itching to do that. If so, that will give us even more time. And if the Envoy relaxes enough to stop monitoring Jeremiah's brain—which is likely—I can then deal with Jeremiah's wish to get rid of you by using the resources I currently have. This is only a contingency on the off chance that you're *unable* to stop the Test. If you succeed with the Test, we'll have a ton more options."

"I like that," I think, mulling over her long explanation. "But what about Fiona? What will happen to her if they think she's guilty?"

"If the Lens of Truth doesn't clear her, you mean? I guess Jeremiah will grant her what she wanted anyway. He'll kick her off the Council."

"But—"

"Look, if you're so concerned about her, I have this other idea based on something you said, but don't worry about it for now."

"Okay," I think, feeling a bit less like one of those ancient lambs going to the slaughter. "Tell me your plan. How do I take this Test?"

As Phoe outlines the start of her crazy plan, I rethink my sense of relief. If I *were* a lamb, I wouldn't be just going to the slaughter; I'd be picking a fight with a wolf right before entering the slaughterhouse.

CHAPTER TEN

I walk back to the Birth Day celebrations. It takes me some time, but I finally spot the perfect group of people for what Phoe has in mind.

There, by a tent, the Dean and a few other people who work with him are speaking with professional tennis players.

As luck would have it, there aren't many Youths around them. That's good. I'd rather my peers not witness what I'm about to do, since word might reach Liam and I'd have a hard time explaining this to him—or anyone else, for that matter.

I confidently stroll to the middle of the dozen or so people.

They look at me curiously.

I inhale a good amount of air into my lungs.

The Dean seems on a verge of saying hello, but he never gets the chance to speak.

As loudly as I can, I say, "Fuck. Vagina. Shit."

The silence that follows reminds me of the calm that preluded ancient storms. Even the distant sounds of music seem muted.

"I lost a bet," I say to the petrified Dean. "Don't worry. I'll make my way to the Quietude building."

As I walk away, I say every other obscene word I can think of. I do this at a much quieter volume than my introduction, but loud enough for the Dean to hear. After a few choice words, I find it surprisingly hard to keep this up. As I get farther away, I'm convinced I've repeated myself at least a couple times. Still, it's not originality that counts, but the quality of the words. On a few occasions, I cheat by combining words I already mentioned with other forbidden and even mundane words, getting pretty creative with the combinations. Phoe is laughing so hard she's holding her stomach, but she still manages to give me a few suggestions—words the Dean will probably have to look up in an anatomy book, if he isn't too preoccupied with his wilting ears.

What's particularly funny, in a purely morbid sort of way, is that no one stops me as I go. They keep their distance and don't utter a single word as I walk toward the Witch Prison of my own volition.

I assume the Dean, or one of the other Adults, gathered his wits shortly after I left, because after a few minutes, a Guard heads my way from the pentagonal prism that is my destination.

"This is going great so far," I subvocalize as sarcastically as I can. "You sure I shouldn't have gotten naked, covered myself with tar, and rolled around in some feathers?"

"I think it would've helped if you had licked the Dean's bald head like I suggested," Phoe says, still chuckling. "But I think even without that, we got the point across."

I give her a chiding look, but that only adds to her merriment.

As the Guard gets closer to me, however, Phoe grows serious again.

"Remember, I'll have a hard time getting in touch with you once you're in the Witch Prison," she reminds me. "I figured out how to see through the Guards' cameras, but that's still fairly limited—"

"And we hope the Envoy will have similar troubles," I repeat, my mental voice a parody of hers. "Isn't that why I'm doing this crazy stunt to begin with?"

"Even if the Envoy can see everything that happens inside the Quietude building—which I doubt—my plan should still work, assuming the Envoy is not all-knowing and all-seeing," Phoe says. "And if he *were* all-knowing and all-seeing, we'd be dead already. The Faraday cage of that building provides us an extra bonus, because if he *can't* see inside, it turns a good plan into a great one."

Since I know what the plan *is*, I can't help but mutter some more curses, this time as a way to show my opinion on the 'greatness' of this so-called plan.

When I meet the Guard, he stands there, arms folded over his chest, and says nothing.

With disappointment, I note that this Guard is much too short and stocky for what we need. He's closer to Liam's build than mine. That means I'll have to work with a slightly more complicated version of an already-dubious plan.

"I'll go with you," I say, failing to not sound belligerent. "Lead the way."

The Guard gestures.

"I can't believe he tried to Pacify you!" Phoe exclaims. "These people really do abuse their power."

I stay quiet and do my best impersonation of getting Pacified. Having actually felt this when Jeremiah did it to me helps my acting.

The Guard is convinced enough by my performance to turn around and head in the direction of our intended destination.

As we walk, Phoe repeats the remaining steps of the plan. If I weren't pretending to be Pacified, I'd be screaming obscenities again.

"Good luck," Phoe says as we're about to enter the Prison. "I know you'll do great."

"Thanks," I think grumpily. "I hope you're right."

We walk in.

Phoe doesn't talk anymore, but I derive comfort from the knowledge that I'm not completely on my own. She got me out of here the day before yesterday.

After walking the maze-like corridors, we reach a nondescript door, and the Guard gestures.

The door to the room opens.

The Guard stands in the corridor expectantly.

I walk in, and he closes the door, locking me in.

So far so good—or at least, according to plan.

I look at the table and whistle. There are three bars of tasteless Prison Food. That means, under normal circumstances, I'd be stuck in this room for at least three days.

I walk back to the door and count to a thousand to make sure the Guard who brought me here is gone.

When I put my ear to the door and listen, I hear nothing.

A ghostly Screen appears in the air next to me.

A cursor flickers on the Screen, and a single character shows up and types the letter 'G.' Then the second one appears with the letter 'O.'

I make an okay sign in case Phoe can see me and wave my hand at the door in the standard 'open' gesture.

The door unlocks with a loud *click*.

This first part of the plan didn't even require Phoe's help. All I did was use my newly acquired Elderly access.

Annoyingly, the Screen now says: *I told you so.*

I shake my head and walk out of the room.

The Screen follows me. On it, Phoe types out: *Two lefts and a right.* When I make the first turn, the Screen flickers and disappears.

I walk down the next corridor, making sure to turn carefully when I reach the end.

The second left takes me down a winding corridor that looks like the one we passed when the Guard brought me in here. I could be wrong, though. All the corridors in this place look the same in their washed-out grayness.

Before I turn right, I crouch and look around the corner. My target is where he should be, and this Guard matches both my height and weight.

Great. Finally something is going my way.

The Guard is leisurely walking away from me, so all I see is his back.

This is actually good news.

The bad news is that, according to Phoe's estimations, I have to get closer, within six feet to be precise, to execute the next part of the plan.

I enter the corridor as slowly and softly as I can. My feet are barely touching the floor.

The problem with approaching the Guard stealthily is that I'm moving at the same speed as him. If I keep this up, I'll never catch up with him.

I take longer strides, trying my best to keep quiet.

The ghostly Screen shows up again and asks: *What's the holdup?*

I walk a few more steps and decide the distance between us should be sufficient.

As I stop, my shoes make a barely noticeable rustle against the floor.

There should be no way the Guard heard it, yet he slows his pace.

Crap.

He heard me.

"Oh well," I think in case Phoe can hear me. "It won't matter in a moment anyway."

I raise my hand the way Phoe instructed me, the way the Guards do when they try to Pacify *me*. Phoe figured out that if I make my wrist flick stronger, the

Pacify effect will be more intense and will nearly knock out the target.

The Guard turns around.

I repeat the gesture.

He's too spry for someone under the effects of the Pacify.

The letters show up frantically on the Screen: *Shit. It didn't work.*

The Screen clears, then says: *They must be protected against another Elderly using Pacify on them, which was unexpected.* The Screen clears again, then in very big font: *Why are you still standing there? Abort mission and run.*

"You said this was a great plan," I think angrily at the Screen.

Run already.

The Guard is a leap away.

I'm not sure running will be *that* effective, so I decide to improvise.

"My door just opened," I say to him in a meek voice. "I stepped out and got lost."

The Guard performs his own Pacify gesture at me as he reaches for the Stun Stick on his belt.

Why is he going for that Stick? Does he know Pacify didn't work? Or did he see my attempt to Pacify him?

I slump as though I'm Pacified.

At the same time, through my half-closed eyelids, I watch his hand.

He's still reaching for that Stick, leaving me little choice.

I have to attack the Guard.

As I mentally prepare for what I have to do, I can't help but feel a sense of déjà vu. I confronted a Guard inside the nightmarish vision of the IRES game. *That* fight didn't go so well for me. I would've died had it not been for the in-game History Instructor driving a tractor into him, something I'm pretty sure can't happen *now*.

The Screen shows up in the air again with a very pertinent message: *Act.*

I stop thinking and become motion. As quickly as I can, I squat and sweep my right leg around, hoping to bring the Guard down to the floor.

The Guard jumps.

Fighting panic, I jump back up and prepare to rush him.

The Guard takes out his Stun Stick and fiddles with its controls. I use his momentary distraction to ram my shoulder into his midsection.

The Stun Stick falls out of his hands, but I can't tell if it's from pain or the kinetic energy of my impact. With his helmet on, it's hard to tell what my opponent is feeling or where he's looking, which puts me at a big disadvantage.

My hit didn't slow him down much, though, because seamlessly, he slams his fist into the side of my head.

My ear explodes with burning pain.

I grit my teeth and ignore the blood pounding in my temples. I channel the anger flooding through my system into a not-so-gentlemanly maneuver I also utilized against that virtual Guard.

My leg goes up, and my foot connects with the crotch area of the Guard's white outfit.

If the pain in my foot is any indication, the kick was strong. Had this been a soccer game, the ball would've flown far beyond the field.

The Guard stops.

Again, the visor makes it hard to see how I did, but I'm hoping the stop means he's in pain.

Capitalizing on my success, I put my right foot behind the man's ankle and push.

I'm hoping he trips and falls. When I used this trick back in kindergarten, Owen certainly fell.

The jerky motion and my foot's odd position almost tip *me* over, but the Guard keeps his balance as though his feet are glued to the gray floor.

And just when I think things can't get any worse, they do.

The Guard sidesteps, and before I fully understand what's happening, my neck ends up in a chokehold between the Guard's forearm and bicep.

Blood drains from my face.

I've seen this scenario in movies. It typically involves the hero sneaking up on the bad guy in an attempt to get rid of him silently. It never ends well for the bad guy.

The Guard squeezes.

I grab his arm to pry it away.

It's like trying to pry apart welded pieces of steel.

Fighting panic, I attempt to inhale.

Nothing.

The Guard's chokehold is preventing air from entering my lungs.

CHAPTER ELEVEN

I kick backward, but the Guard dodges. I stomp on his foot, but the white spacesuit shoes must have steel toes, because he shows no sign that I hurt him. Instead, the Guard tightens his grip. My squirming doesn't have any effect on him.

After struggling for a few seconds, I realize something rather odd. Though I haven't taken a breath in at least thirty seconds, I'm handling the oxygen deprivation relatively well. In the IRES version of this fight, when the imaginary Guard choked me, my vision went white and I became faint almost immediately. Granted, that was a simulated experience and the Guard was using his hands, not this elbow grip, but given the game's ultra-realism, I imagine the principle of choking someone to death would hold, and if so, I should be feeling what I felt then. Why isn't it happening? Why do I feel relatively okay, with no signs that I'm about to pass out and die?

Then I remember the Respirocytes—the nano machines Phoe turned on inside my body. Naturally, when she returned my memory, she reactivated everything else, including that technology.

That must explain why I'm still okay, but without consulting Phoe, I have no idea how long I'll last.

I'm not even sure if the Guard is blocking my air supply or the flow of blood to my brain. If it's the latter, it might be bad. I can go a long time without air, but I'm less sure about having my blood flow restricted. The Respirocytes travel through my bloodstream, so even they can't save me from blacking out if I stay in this position long enough—however long that is.

I formulate a quick plan.

Acting like someone who's running out of energy, I lazily tug at the Guard's forearm.

He keeps his hold on my neck.

I have no idea how long I've been in his grip or how much time it would take for a normal person to get so weak they'd stop fighting, but I hope the Guard doesn't know those statistics either. It's not something that's useful in our violence-free society.

I slow my movements.

He doesn't let go.

I let my body go slack, pretending to pass out.

The Guard keeps his hold on my neck.

My panic reaches new heights. If my bluff doesn't work, he might stand here long enough to choke me to death—with or without the Respirocytes.

I fight the panic and the need to stiffen my body. I keep my limbs relaxed, the way someone who's lost consciousness would.

Then I genuinely begin to feel faint, and with that, the panic returns with exponential intensity. In another second, I won't be able to stand here, slack, pretending to be passed out. I'll be forced to fight again.

The Guard loosens his grip and lowers me to the ground, careful not to drop me.

Through the slit in my eyelids, I spot the Stun Stick.

If I reach with my right hand, I might get it, but I'd give away my true condition. The problem is, he still has me in that chokehold.

I stall as the Guard lays me on my stomach and lets go of my neck.

Surreptitiously, I take a small inhale.

Though my lungs feel unsatisfyingly empty, I know I can rely on the Respirocyte technology to keep me oxygenated.

The Guard grabs my left arm and pulls it to the right.

I don't fight him at first, but when I feel something click on my left wrist, I decide not to wait any longer. As swiftly as I can, I push up off the ground and leap for the Stun Stick.

Whatever the Guard snapped around my left wrist tightens painfully, and I realize I'm tethered to the Guard somehow. Reaching out with my free hand, I stretch my fingers to grasp the handle of the Stun Stick.

The Guard pulls on the thing tethering us together.

My left arm threatens to pop out of its socket, but my fingers close around the Stun Stick.

Swallowing a scream, I shove the Stun Stick into the Guard's thigh and squeeze the button so hard the bones in my thumb crack.

The Guard slumps against me.

Sucking in a lungful of air, I turn around.

The thing on my left arm is some kind of handcuff, though instead of being made of metal, as depicted in ancient media, these are made of the same dull gray material as the Witch Prison's walls. The Guard was holding on to the second cuff right up until I zapped him. I was lucky he never finished cuffing my right arm, or else I'd be toast.

I fiddle with the handcuff, but it doesn't yield.

The ghostly Screen shows up in the air and tells me: *Gesture for it to open the way you would a door. Then do the same to the Guard's helmet.*

I gesture hysterically at the cuffs.

Both the cuff on my hand and its empty cousin open with a loud *click*.

Emboldened, I repeat the motion at the Guard's helmet.

There's a hollow *whoosh* sound, and a gap appears between the Guard's helmet and the neckpiece of his white outfit.

As a precaution, I unload another Stun Stick charge into him. He doesn't react.

Content with my victim's passivity, I take off his helmet.

The man's eyes are closed and his hawkish features are calm, as though he's taking a nap. His hair is mostly black, with only the beginning of gray at his temples. Like the other Guards, he looks like a younger Elderly. I hope that'll allow him to survive the boatload of Stun Stick zappings coming his way.

I put aside the helmet and work on taking off the rest of his suit.

Phoe's plan, for all its craziness, is simple: to make sure no one recognizes me as I make my way to the Elderly section, I'll dress as a Guard. It worked for Fiona and Jeremiah, so the same idea should work for me. The crazy part was the cursing-assisted Quietude, plus the actual act of getting the Guard to give up his suit.

When I finish with the man's boots, I begin to undress instead of disappearing my clothes with a gesture, so I can leave the Guard dressed in something rather than naked.

Before I put on the Guard's suit, I zap him with the Stick to make sure he stays knocked out.

I put on the helmet, and the world becomes dimmer but with a bunch of overlaying visualizations. This helmet has something like a Screen built into the visor. As cool as it is, I don't dare play with it, at least not until I bring Phoe's plan to its conclusion.

Haphazardly, I put my old clothes on the unconscious man. Then, using his handcuffs, I cuff his hands behind his back and make a 'close' gesture.

The restraints seem to stay put.

Now the hardest part begins. I drag the unconscious Elderly by his legs and pause every so often to zap him. I'm not sure if it's from my adrenaline or the Respirocytes, but backtracking to my room isn't as exhausting as I imagined.

When I get back to my designated Quietude room, I drag the Guard inside and thoughtfully put him on the bed. I zap him one last time, put the Stun Stick on my belt, and exit the room.

This is the last part of Phoe's plan.

I make a door-closing gesture, and the door slams shut.

There's a locking sound, then an unusual crunching noise. Phoe said she would jam the door once it was closed, so I assume that's what the crunch was about.

The ghostly Screen comes to life and confirms that the door is jammed. It also informs me of where I should go to make sure I don't run into any of 'my fellow Guards.'

I run the whole way, which makes my trip *out* of the Prison last about a minute.

"Phoe?" I think as soon as I exit the final door. "Is this helmet preventing you from talking to me?"

"Not at all," Phoe says, her voice coming from my right.

I turn and see her standing there, grinning as she looks me up and down.

"Your helmet isn't attached," she says and makes a closing motion with her hand.

I hear a click around my neck, and the controls in my visor really come to life.

A map of Oasis appears in my peripheral vision, as well as a million other inputs I don't understand.

To top it off, the air smells different, ozone-like.

"That's because you're wearing an actual space suit." Phoe's voice sounds like it's coming from somewhere inside my helmet. "My guess is, a while back, the Elderly repurposed the spacesuits that came with the Ship. It makes sense. Unlike most other clothes in Oasis, these suits were manufactured on Earth and not via nano assembly, so no one 'malicious,' like you or I, can recreate one with a gesture. I guess they also figured it would be helpful for the police force to have a distinctive look, not to mention the many helpful functions of the suit." Her grin widens. "These suits take care of the wearer's bodily functions and needs so a Guard can focus on—"

"Yuck." I wrinkle my nose. "You're telling me the Guard used this suit as a bathroom?"

She looks thoughtful for a moment, then says, "I just examined the suit's sensors. It's as close to a sterile environment as it gets. You have nothing to worry about."

"Okay," I say, trying hard not to think about the suit as a toilet. "What now?"

"Walk toward the Adult section." Phoe points in the direction of the pine forest. "Though my door-jamming trick worked, we don't know how much time we have. If the Envoy is somehow keeping an eye on the Prison—"

"Didn't you say I have to be the last person to take the Elderly Test? Isn't that the only way to make sure no one notices its absence for a year?" I ask as I walk toward the forest. "It's not evening yet."

"This is why we're taking our time getting there." Phoe walks next to me with a cheerful spring in her step. "I was thinking we could wait in the forest by the Barrier on the Adult side of Oasis until sunset."

"Isn't that dangerous?" I glance at her. "Even in this disguise, if we come across another Guard, they might ask me something, and I'd be screwed."

"True," Phoe says. "Which is why we should do our best not to run into any Guards. Fortunately, your nifty new suit has all sorts of sensors that can help us." She makes a gesture, and I suddenly see the world in blue and red colors.

"That's heat vision," Phoe explains and returns my vision to normal. "In that mode, you can see people behind trees, long before they get the chance to see you."

"Cool," I think. "That *should* help."

"Yep, it should, and there's another thing I want to do," Phoe says. "Something that will allow me to keep you safe, but I'm afraid you won't like it."

"My list of dislikes is growing, that's for sure. What is it this time? I know you'll tell me anyway. You just want me to want you to tell me."

"Just keep an open mind, please," she says with a slight pout.

"Fine, I will. Come out with it already."

"Okay." Phoe stops and looks at me. "I want to ride your body."

CHAPTER TWELVE

My cheeks and the tips of my ears get uncomfortably warm. I've seen enough ancient movies to understand that expression. Riding someone means—

"Great, now that your hormones are normalizing, you're turning into a horndog." Phoe puts her hands on her hips. "Whether I want intimacy has nothing to do with what I'm talking about. You're thinking of the innuendo, but I'm speaking more literally. I want to ride your body the way I rode Jeremiah the other day, when I had him untie you."

"You mean when he was moving like a puppet?" I subvocalize. My blush disappears as blood leaves my face. Instinctively, I increase my pace, as if trying to run away from Phoe.

"Perhaps that wasn't the best reminder," she says, hurrying to catch up with me. "Jeremiah was moving erratically because I hadn't mastered the interface between the nanos and the neurons in the motor cortex, which made that episode a little unnerving. I have since been looking into perfecting that interface, as well as involving more brain regions, such as the cerebellum, parts of the frontal lobe, and the basal ganglia. I believe I can take over walking and running for you, and do it so smoothly it will be indistinguishable from your own behavior."

I stop walking and consider this. Somehow the idea that I wouldn't be moving in jerky motions makes me feel a bit better about this proposition.

"But why?" I think to myself and to Phoe. "Why do you want to control my body like that?"

"When we get to the Testing facility, once you initiate the Test like every other VR session, your consciousness will not be present in your body.

Given the tight security and the Envoy situation, I don't want you standing there like a statue."

"Hmm," I think and resume walking. "I haven't thought that far ahead. When you put it like that, it sounds like a good idea."

"Yeah, and I promise it won't feel unpleasant, if that's what you're worried about," she says and also starts walking.

"If my mind is busy with VR, I won't feel anything anyway," I think.

"True, but I want to test it out while you're present in your mind. You see, this isn't just for VR. There are other interesting possibilities. For example, say I see you're in danger. Right now, I'd have to tell you, which takes time. If I mastered this skill, and you gave me permission, I could move your body away from the danger on my own, which might save your life, but I need to make sure you're okay with me doing this when you're still conscious of it."

I walk silently for a few minutes, considering her proposal. At the core, my reservations about this idea are irrational. I fear Phoe taking away my control, but that's silly. If she wanted to do that, she would have. Instead, she's asking for permission.

"Fear of technology is so ingrained in you that I can't blame you for being wary." Phoe's tone is almost tender.

"Let's try it," I subvocalize firmly, mostly out of a sense of rebellion. I always want to do the opposite of what the Adults are trying to brainwash me to do.

"Okay," Phoe thinks. "Ready?"

"Do it," I think.

I keep walking.

Nothing happens for at least twenty steps.

"So?" Phoe says. "That wasn't so bad, was it?"

"What are you talking about? You didn't do anything." I examine my legs and arms and find that they're completely under my control.

"I took control," Phoe says. "First with every other step, and then all the steps between the eighth and the fifteenth."

"You were walking for me some of the time? But I didn't feel it."

"Your brain must be trying to sustain the illusion of free will," Phoe says thoughtfully. "I've read about that. It's a form of confabulation."

"Or it didn't work," I think, more to myself.

I stop.

"Why did you stop?" Phoe asks, her voice taunting, almost challenging.

I think back.

It was just one of those spur of the moment decisions. I wanted to stop, at least that's how it felt.

"Except *I* made you stop." Phoe holds her hand out to stop my objections and says, "How about this?"

My gloved hand smacks the visor of my helmet.

It's a strange sensation, like maybe I wanted to do that, yet I'm beginning to doubt myself.

Then I notice I'm hopping on one foot.

"Okay, Phoe, I believe you. Please stop humiliating me," I say, picturing what I would think if I ever saw a Guard hopping like this. Once my feet are planted firmly on the ground, I add, "This isn't what I expected at all. If anything, it's less scary than what I feared. I thought it would be like the Lens of Truth, like I'd be a spectator trapped outside my body."

"I just read some literature on the subject, and I'm not that surprised by your reaction anymore. Willful control over muscles is a very strange thing for human beings. Studies have proven that certain actions and behaviors begin *before* people consciously realize they're doing them. That is, muscle activity starts before individuals press the button indicating they feel like moving that muscle. Many actions happen on autopilot, like yanking a hand away from a hot object. I suspect that when I do something minor, like taking over your walk, your consciousness assumes you're still in control. When it's something you have no reason to do, then we get into interesting territory. Oh, and by the way, did you notice that as I was speaking, I was walking for you?"

I stop and think about whether I was consciously controlling my legs. It's hard to say. Walking can be done quite mindlessly at times.

"All right, Phoe. If you wanted to make me feel comfortable with this process, you're on the right track. What do you want to try next?"

"We should test this closer to the actual scenario I'm worried about, with your mind in VR and me controlling you," Phoe says. "Why don't you go into your man cave while I keep walking for you?"

Without hesitation, I make the requisite gesture, and the white tunnel takes me to my man cave.

Phoe is already standing there, between an old cannon and something that looks like a guillotine. She extends her palm and initiates a hologram-like image that shows me walking toward the forest in the real world.

"Your gait looks good," she says, looking at the video feed.

She's right. I look like a Guard who's casually walking toward the forest. The movements aren't jerky or too slow. The steps my body is taking under Phoe's control are indistinguishable from my own.

"You know, it's really odd that you're here talking to me while you're controlling my legs," I tell Phoe.

"I don't see why. I'm also monitoring Fiona and Jeremiah's interviews, reading a bunch of books, researching whatever I can about the Test, getting the details of the egg hunt they're having in the forest to make sure we don't bump into anyone, and—"

"I get it," I say, doing my best not to sound envious. "You can multitask."

"I don't actually have to multitask in the 'doing many things at the same time' sense. Given that I think much faster than human beings, I simply perform each task linearly. For example, I can finish a book in a fraction of a millisecond, then check in on the interviews, and all before your meat brain fires a single synapse. Of course, I also do multitask. There are multiple versions of me—"

"I don't understand," I say. "Are you actually here with me or not?" I walk over and touch her shoulder. Here, in the VR environment she's created for me, I'm dressed in my Birth Day outfit of jeans and a t-shirt, not the Guard suit, and my bare hand feels her shoulder with no obstacles. She feels completely real—soft and warm to the touch.

"Of course I'm here," Phoe says. "And before you insult me by asking, I can feel you touching my shoulder."

"Phoe, I—"

"It's okay, Theo," she says, her blue eyes piercing mine. "You have the right to understand this. When I take this shape"—she runs the tips of her fingers down her body—"the thread of me you're communicating with is not merely *pretending* to have this body. This part of me actually has a body or as close to that as possible in the given medium. In VR, this body you see is an emulation of a human one. Emulation is a process where I replicate something with as much detail as I can. In this form, I have neurons, dendrites, blood, a heart, nerves, hormones, as well as gut bacteria. If it's possible to capture the totality of the human experience in a virtual way—and I believe that it *is* possible—then I have done so. So you see, at a minimum, this allows me to feel everything a human being can feel. It allows me to be here with you, both in terms of sensations and emotions."

I open my mouth to ask more questions, but she doesn't give me a chance. "And yes," she says, "I'm capable of more than just physical sensations. My emotions run much deeper and are more nuanced than a human being's because I'm not limited to just this body—no matter how complex my emulated brain is. My capacity for compassion is higher, and my understanding of the world is richer." She gives me a level look. "A question you need to ask yourself is: Are *you* capable of human emotions? I know you felt my shoulder with the tips of your fingers, and I know your oxytocin levels went up minutely when you touched me, but did it make you feel happy, the way a human being should feel when touching a friend? Or was your capacity to feel such things destroyed by years of Quietudes and the brain-tampering of the Oasis society?"

I stare at her uncomprehendingly. She doesn't blink. She truly thinks she's more human than I am—she, an AI.

"I am, though," she says. "But you'll get there. You're on your way to being fully human too."

And before I can reply, she stands on her tiptoes and kisses me.

CHAPTER THIRTEEN

Our kiss is almost angry in its intensity. The warmth of her body presses against me, and I get the urge to pull her closer, to touch her and get rid of the clothes between us.

Before I can do so, she gently pushes me away and says, "Hold your horses, Theo. I don't think you know what you're feeling or fully understand what you want. Until you do, we should take the physical part of our whatever-this-is slowly."

I'm a muddy roller coaster of needs and emotions, with Phoe at the epicenter. Her words sound far away, their meaning fuzzy, but she's right. I don't know much about whatever it is I want from her.

"Look," she says, turning my attention to the hologram of me walking.

I look, even though I know she's just changing the topic.

The real-world me is in the forest. He/I/we are walking briskly.

"'We' is a fitting pronoun," Phoe says, once again composed. "Since it's your body we're looking at, yet it's me controlling it. I'll get it to the Barrier for you, okay?"

"Fine. What do we do in the meantime?" I ask, the image of more kissing flitting through my mind.

Phoe chuckles slyly and says, "For starters, you can accept your Birth Day present." She turns to walk deeper into the cave.

I follow her. "My present?" I ask.

"Oh, right." She glances over her shoulder. "I keep forgetting that Birth Day is but a shallow echo of ancients' birthdays. You see, unlike Oasis, where thanks to artificial wombs and Incubators, everyone is born on the same day, the ancients were born at random times. So they felt special and wanted gifts to commemorate—"

"I'm well aware of the idea of a birthday gift," I say as we stop next to a table with two chairs. "I just got caught off guard."

Phoe grins at me. "Okay. Well, I prepared this for you."

The table is covered with every ancient food and drink I've ever tasted on Birth Day. There are several flavors of soda and popcorn and a dozen other goodies. A big bowl of fried dough sits as the centerpiece of the table.

"I had to stick to things you'd tasted before, or else I would've had to make up the textures and flavors, which I *could* do, if you wanted."

Instead of responding, I grab a piece of fried dough and pop it in my mouth. Phoe follows my lead. The taste is identical to the way I remember it, and I simply let myself enjoy it.

Once I'm done chewing, I say, "Thank you. This is awesome."

"You can eat as many as you want without getting sick." She winks at me. "I'm not emulating *your* digestive track, so you're eating virtual ether."

"So"—I take a piece of popcorn from a paper bag—"if your body is such a good emulation of a human one, can you get fat from eating too much fried dough?"

"Theo, Theo," she says and follows it with a *tsk-tsk* sound. "It's not gentlemanly to ask a lady about her age, and even less so to allude to her weight."

"It's not?" I grab a piece of fried dough and lick the powdered sugar off it.

"It was an ancient tradition," Phoe says and demonstratively stuffs a bunch of fried dough into her mouth. She must have swallowed it without chewing, because she soon continues. "But I was actually teasing you. If you think my butt is fat, please tell me, because I can make it smaller. Just because I try to emulate everything accurately doesn't mean I can't take some liberties when I feel like it."

I take a noisy gulp of soda, then say, "You can look any way you wish?"

Phoe nods. "Yes, and more importantly, I can look any way *you* wish." And before my stunned gaze, her eyes switch from their usual blue to green and then back again. At the same time, her blond pixie hair turns pink, then returns to blond. "I created this face by studying your pupil dilation and other cues when you watched ancient movies and gawked at the models in those magazines. I tried to look like the perfect woman for you, but if you wanted, I could look different, say like your friend Grace"—there's a dark undertone to her voice as she says this—"or like anyone else."

"I like you like this," I say, putting the large soda back on the table. "Please don't change, and please refrain from manipulating me in such a crude fashion in the future. I can't believe you made yourself look like the girls I stared at. That's just unfair."

"That's why I came clean." Phoe reaches for the cup I was holding, her fingers momentarily touching mine. "I realized it was manipulative, and I felt guilty about it. In my defense, I had to make myself look like *something*, so why not look pleasing to you?" She bats her eyelashes at me. "Do you forgive me?"

I watch those long lashes flutter and wonder if she borrowed that action from some movie after seeing how it affected me. Even with that suspicion in mind,

I find I can't be mad at her for longer than a few seconds.

"Good." Phoe grins, then takes two bags of popcorn, hands one to me, and says, "Let's watch some movies while we wait for your body to reach its destination."

She walks to a far crevice of the cave, and I follow. When we arrive, I see that Phoe has managed to create a full-fledged ancient movie theater. We sit down with our popcorn—ancient moviegoer style—and watch a couple of films.

By the third movie, I figure out Phoe's agenda. She's showing me romantic comedies to teach me human courting behavior and vernacular. I don't mind, though. It's actually interesting. Ancients had a very strange relationship with sexual intimacy. They clearly loved to have sex, but had a harder time talking about it, almost as though they followed some of Oasis's taboos. Many of them went as far as to use baseball as a metaphor for sex instead of talking directly about it. Using this euphemism, Phoe and I went to 'first base.' I have to hand it to the ancients for their creativity. Thinking of what we did as 'first base' doesn't make me nearly as uncomfortable as thinking of it as 'kissing.'

"That's good to know." Phoe makes the movie screen disappear and leans toward me. "I'm glad you saw through my ploy." She flicks her fingers, and the movie theater chairs disappear. We're suddenly sitting on a couch, surrounded by candles and that distinctly romantic music from the movies we watched. "As your reward for your cleverness, perhaps I'll let you convince me to go to 'second base.'"

Having just seen what that means from one of the movies, I reach for her, my heart beating faster than those times I almost died. We go at it for what feels like hours, and by the end, I have a renewed appreciation for what drove the ancients mad.

* * *

I fix my hair and my clothes as I walk back to the central part of the cave, where I appeared what feels like a month ago, back when I was innocent and pure.

Phoe follows me.

I reach the hologram and gaze at myself in the real world.

"Is that the forest on the Adult side?" I ask. He/we are surrounded by pines. It's sundown, and I have to assume we've had sufficient time to get through the Youth's pine forest, cross the Barrier, and enter the forest on the other side.

Phoe licks her lips. I catch myself staring at them. They look puffy after what we've done.

She catches me looking, winks, and says, "That's correct. We should be able to get on with our quest soon, unless you want to hang out here while I fly the disk myself . . ."

"Fly a disk? You never mentioned we'd be flying." I suppress a shudder. "Can I just walk?"

"Adults are still celebrating Birth Day." Phoe gestures, and two chairs appear. "They have a big hoopla, just like Youths. Our chances of running into someone are greater on foot."

I sit on my chair and say, "I think it might be worth the risk—"

"You don't even have to be conscious of the flying." Phoe drags her chair next to mine, sits down, and gives my arm a sympathetic pat. "We can stay here and hang out while I—my thread on the outside—do the flying."

"No." I notice my feet pointing away from the hologram as though I'm planning to run away. "I'll do it. I need to get over my fear of heights."

"As you wish." Phoe crosses her legs. "You'll have the option of letting me take over at any time."

"How is your investigation progressing?" I ask, desperate to get my mind off the subject of heights. "Is Jeremiah still questioning people?"

"No, that finished hours ago. He and Fiona are actually almost back in the Elderly section. They flew on disks like the other Guards do when traveling outside the Youth section. And before you ask, they haven't spoken about you or your neural scan since that terse conversation. I don't know if that's a good sign, since they haven't spoken much at all. It's clear they're disappointed by the lack of information. I think they're considering their options. Things should get interesting once Jeremiah discovers the video of Fiona, but he hasn't yet. Which reminds me . . ." Phoe rubs her palms together excitedly. "There's something I neglected to show you."

I raise an eyebrow in question, and she brings up a huge Screen in front of us.

On the Screen is the Council meeting. The room looks identical to the one Phoe showed me earlier, the one where Fiona tried to quit the Council.

The camera zooms in on Jeremiah, who's standing next to Fiona, like in the other videos.

Jeremiah's features are the epitome of wrath. I cringe, realizing I've seen this expression on his face before, but I can't recall exactly when.

"When he tortured you," Phoe whispers and rubs my shoulder.

She might be right. In this scenario, his anger is focused on a new target: Fiona.

"You fucking bitch," Jeremiah says with such venom that I move away, pressing into the back of my chair.

Fiona seems petrified as she watches Jeremiah raise his hand. The rest of the Council members' faces are marble white.

The back of Jeremiah's withered hand travels toward Fiona's right cheek, almost in slow motion.

I hear a loud slap, and Fiona staggers backward, her hands protecting her head.

I can't believe what I saw.
Jeremiah smacked Fiona in the face.

CHAPTER FOURTEEN

The Screen goes black.

I stare, completely dumbfounded.

Jeremiah may have done many terrible things, but these actions are beyond anything I expected to see. That an Elderly would break the vulgarity and violence taboos is unthinkable.

"You think I overdid it?" Phoe asks, her fingers in a steeple in front of her chest.

"What do you mean you overdid it?" I blink at my friend, who looks too happy given what we just saw.

"Oh, you thought that was real?" Phoe's smile widens. "That's excellent news. If you thought it was real, so will everyone else."

"That *wasn't* real?" I scratch the back of my head. "He didn't smack her?"

"Remember when you said Fiona might accuse Jeremiah of faking that video I dug up? The one where she almost quit the Council? I replied that Jeremiah would say he couldn't fake a video. Your question, however, gave me an idea. Since *I* can do something like that, why not create a video that would compromise Jeremiah? Why not depict him doing something he'd want the others to Forget? And if that action took place during a Council meeting, that would explain where the memory of that meeting went." She leans forward in her chair. "So I did just that. It wasn't even all that hard. Judging by your reaction, I take it that it looks pretty authentic. This should really help us divide and conquer them."

I look at Phoe. Shaking my head, I say, "I'm glad you're on my side. If the Elderly knew what you could do, I think they'd feel justified in having been afraid of AIs all this time."

"I use my power for good." Phoe puts her hands behind her head and beams at me. "And I try to use it as little as possible. I thought you were worried about Fiona and what will happen once Jeremiah sees the video that compromises *her*. This way, as soon as she gets into trouble, I can make sure she comes across *this* video. It'll give her ammunition against Jeremiah's accusations."

"So long as no one focuses on the two of us, I say you did the right thing," I subvocalize. Then I remember I can speak freely in my cave and say out loud, "It's just a little creepy, that's all, him smacking her like that."

"Should I change his actions? I could show him projectile vomiting and thrashing around the room, like a scene from *The Exorcist*." Phoe stands and makes her eyes go white as she extends her arms like a zombie. "I bet that's how many of the Elderly picture insanity."

"No." I suppress a wave of nausea. "Or if you do create a video like that, please make it a point to *not* show me."

"Spoilsport." Phoe's eyes return to normal, and she sits down. "I think I'll stick with this version of the video. Now, I just have to tell you this one last thing . . ." She stops. "Actually, since you brought up scary powers and all that, perhaps it can wait."

"What is it?" I narrow my eyes. "Why do I have a feeling you're about to tell me something I *really* won't like?"

"It's about the Test." Phoe brings her knees closer together. "I've been unable to hack into the place where the Test runs, which means my only way in is physical—when you access it."

"Right. Wasn't that the plan from the get-go?"

"I was hoping I could learn something about the Test first." She shrugs. "But I couldn't, apart from the instructions every person who's about to take the Test receives."

I catch her gaze. "So what's the problem? Spit it out already."

"Okay, here's the thing." Phoe gives me an uncomfortable look. "Our best bet is to use a Trojan ploy."

"Is that supposed to mean something to me?"

"The Greeks built a giant wooden horse that housed soldiers, and the greedy Trojans pulled it into their sieged city." She sees my eyes glaze over and says, "Never mind. Forget the Trojans. I'm talking about a subterfuge where, by giving you access to the Test, the Test will also, inadvertently, be giving *me* a way inside it."

"That sounds like a great idea. What won't I like about it? The Test should have a problem with this, not me."

"Well, see, since it will be your mind that gains entry into the Test, the backdoor, or the Trojan horse, or whatever we want to call it, has to be part of your mind," Phoe says. "That's what you might not like."

"What?" I turn my chair so we're sitting opposite each other. "Explain."

"It's not *that* bad," she says quickly. "I just need to plant a memory into your mind. A memory that wouldn't be unpleasant."

"Plant a memory?" I slide my chair away from her. "You mean you'd create a fake memory in my head, kind of like that video?"

"Nothing so disturbing as that video, but yeah. Though 'fake' is such a negative word. It would be a tiny alteration of an existing memory. Something that didn't happen to you, per se, but could have."

I cross my arms. “What’s the memory?”

“Oh, nothing terrible. You’ll just remember having done an incredible feat of memorization.” She raises her hand to postpone my follow-up questions. “You will remember having memorized the constant Pi.”

“You mean Pi, as in 3.14-something? The ratio of a circle's circumference to its diameter? Like from Instructor George’s class?” My forehead furrows in confusion. “Is that because it’s a Greek letter and the Trojan thing—”

“No. I chose Pi because some people do take the time to memorize its digits. And because the digits of that number are probably random and go on forever, I can plant a super-long string of digits into your mind without it looking suspicious, at least not to a casual scan like that of the Test. Of course, only the first hundred digits of the number in your head will match the ones from the famous constant. After that cut-off point, the digits won’t be from Pi. They’ll be from Phoe.” She chuckles at her own joke. “They’ll serve their true purpose, which is creating a bootstrapping binary code of devilish design that will—”

"Yes," I interrupt. "Plant the memory if that means you'll stop explaining this."

"Okay," Phoe says and then looks like she's concentrating. She momentarily goes ghostly, the way she did in the real world after I got her the resources from the Zoo. Then she's back to normal and triumphantly says, "Done."

I look at her in shock. I don't feel any different.

"But you do recall memorizing the number Pi?" Her gaze is piercing, as if she's looking inside my head. "Think far back, to ten days ago, when you pretended to be sick. You were sitting in the nurse's office—"

"Wow," I say and stand up. With a sense reminiscent of déjà vu, I recall sitting at the office, bringing up rows and rows of digits on my Screen to memorize them.

"What you really did was play chess with me on your Screen, and you lost so many times you vowed to never play chess with me again."

"Shut up for a second," I say, my voice raised. "Is this a trick?"

Now that the weird feeling is gone, I'm convinced that I chose to study Pi ten days ago at the nurse's office. The idea that I actually played chess with Phoe is so wrong I can't wrap my mind around it. It's simply not what happened. I *did* memorize that stupid number, but I didn't recall it until she reminded me. The memory can't be fake.

"How did you expect a false memory to feel?" Phoe gets up and comes toward me. "If you like, we can play a quick game of chess. You'll lose—badly. You couldn't beat me when I had almost no resources."

"No thanks on the chess, and you're right. I guess this is how it should feel, like I really did memorize that number."

"Please recite the digits for me," Phoe says, her expression turning more serious. She brings up a Screen.

"Three point one four one," I begin. Phoe's Screen shows a large counter that increases by one every time I say another digit.

"That's your position within Pi," Phoe explains. "Keep going."

I recite the digits faster and faster. When the Screen tells us I've reached the hundredth digit in Pi,

Phoe listens intently, and after another few hundred digits, she says, “Okay. It clearly worked.”

“What now?” I ask. “Besides me having a dubious new talent.”

“Now you return to your body and go take the Test.”

“No, I mean, do I have to recite this number when I’m inside the Test? My throat is hoarse from saying the first few hundred numbers, and I probably would—”

“Your throat is not real here, nor will it be during the Test.” Despite her words, Phoe gestures for a glass of water and hands it to me. After I take a sip, she goes on. “But don’t worry, you don’t need to recite it. You can think of this number as a small part of me. Meaning that where you go, a tiny sliver of me goes with you. Once you’re in the Test, or anywhere else that I can’t reach, this number will open a backdoor for more of me to join you.”

“Okay,” I say and drink down the rest of the water. “You got me thinking, though. If the Test scans my brain for memories, won’t it see the memory of you?”

"I doubt it'll scan you so thoroughly. And even if it did, I doubt it would care. The only danger in that scenario would be exposure, but I doubt the Test communicates anything but your score to the outside world. The main reason I even bothered making the numbers in your head look like a natural memory is because the Test might have an internal anti-intrusion algorithm. We don't want to trigger something like that by planting obvious malware in your head, but a subtle memory like this should go unnoticed."

"I see." I rub my eyes. "I think this is the last time I agree to let you mess with my memories. It's too creepy. I remember memorizing those digits so clearly. As boring as losing at chess must've been, it's what really happened, and now that small part of me is gone and it feels wrong."

"I understand," Phoe says, giving me an earnest look. "And I only did it because I had to. Desperate times and all that."

I try to push away my unease and ask, "So what now?"

"Now we should head toward the Elderly section." Phoe emphasizes her suggestion with the double-middle-finger gesture she wants me to make—no doubt a deliberate attempt to shock me out of my anxiety.

Looking at her extended fingers, I realize I've become desensitized to taboos of all sorts. The gesture is nothing compared to what we did on that couch, and I now know that 'second base' is only a glimmer of the things we might do one day. What's even more unfathomable is that I can't wait to go further.

Realizing Phoe probably just read my mind, I flush and hurry to make the necessary gesture to get back to reality.

CHAPTER FIFTEEN

After the usual psychedelic whiteness, I find myself back in the real world.

I'm standing in a little meadow, surrounded by forest on all sides. Dusk has settled, and the first stars are visible above the Dome.

Phoe is already standing on a disk, floating about a foot above the ground.

Next to my feet is my own disk.

I step on it, taken aback by my Guard-issue white pants and boots, since in the cave I was dressed in jeans and sneakers.

"You know the drill," Phoe says and aims her palm upward. Responding to her signal, her disk hovers a few inches higher off the ground.

I tilt my palm at the slightest angle I can get away with, and my disk floats up.

Phoe zips up faster, and in a second, she's as far up as the tips of the tallest pines.

"Come on, join me," she says as a thought in my head. "Or do you need me to literally force your hand?"

I adjust my palm so the disk rises at a steeper angle, while also making a slight forward motion. The only reason my hand isn't shaking is the knowledge that any tiny motion will be translated into movements of the disk, and flying smoothly is terrifying enough.

"There you go," Phoe says when I catch up with her. "You're doing much better."

As though her words jinxed me, I look down. The treetops look like a solid blurry green patch, reminiscent of grass. I can't make out the frightening spaces between the trees.

"That's because I'm taking liberties with Augmented Reality," Phoe admits. "Unless you need to see something below, I figured I'd spare you the adrenaline spike by blurring your view."

"Thanks," I whisper. "Can we fly close to the treetops for now?"

"Sure," she says. "Catch up."

She does something that looks almost like a karate chop from a martial arts movie, and her disk rushes forward so fast I suspect the only reason she doesn't fall off is because she's an AR avatar.

"I'm simulating what would happen with the disk exactly," she says as a disembodied, grumpy voice to my left. "If I were flying for real, this is exactly how it would look."

I push my palm forward as though I'm about to plunge it into boiling water. My disk understands the command as an invitation to go at least ten breathtaking miles per hour.

"Slowpoke," Phoe says once I've caught up to her, a few feet away from the edge of the forest.

"I have a strong sense of self-preservation," I mumble. "Is it safe to fly above more populated areas?"

"It should be in three, two—" Phoe looks at the starry sky. "Now."

I follow her gaze.

The air near the Dome lights up in a gorgeous aurora borealis display.

"I completely forgot about Birth Day," I think, unable to peel my eyes away from the mirage-like colors.

"You've had a long day," Phoe says. "I understand. Hopefully, this explains why no one should notice us, as long as we fly in the areas that do not contain the aurora. No one will be able to look at anything but those lights, and the dark spots in the sky are even darker now. Plus, the bottom of your disk is painted black."

"It might be odd to keep staring up as I fly," I say, still looking at the spectacle.

"You don't need to keep track of the lights. All you need to do is follow me." She starts flying again and says over her shoulder, "I'll take the path no one should see from the ground."

"Is the aurora borealis Augmented Reality?" I ask as I gingerly order my disk to follow her. "I never questioned this before, but I have no idea how the Adults create this spectacle. All I know is that for the ancients, seeing this required visiting Santa at the North Pole and wishing to see something cool."

"Right, visiting Santa. You nailed it." Phoe chuckles. "But to answer your question: yes, that is Augmented Reality, but the fireworks are very real."

Punctuating her words is a roar and a colorful explosion in the distance—the fireworks.

"Great," I think more to myself than Phoe. "I'll be flying through projectiles."

"Oh, how dumb do you think I am?" Though Phoe said it in my head, I can picture her red lips pouting. "Most of my attention is focused on the trajectories of those fireworks."

She stops suddenly and looks left. I stop too and look at what drew her attention.

About a hundred feet away from us is a Guard. He's easy to spot because of the northern lights and the fireworks. His white uniform looks like a rainbow of reflected colors as he hovers in the air on a disk.

"Crap, where did he come from?" I mentally shout at Phoe.

"I'm sorry. He must've been flying above us. I can't scan our surroundings in all three dimensions at all times; the resources that would require—"

"Never mind that. Maybe he didn't see me?" I subvocalize, refusing to succumb to literal wishful thinking.

Something in my helmet makes a strange static noise, and I hear a male voice say, "Noah? Is that you?" The Guard, who I assume is the speaker, flies a foot in my direction. "I thought you drew the short straw and had Quietude duties tonight."

Acting on pure adrenaline, I punch the air with my outstretched hand. The disk rushes away from the approaching Guard with a whoosh of air.

"You did the right thing," Phoe whispers in my head. "Our best course of action is to lose him." Ahead of me, Phoe's disk appears, a reminder that she's not flying for real. "Follow me," she says.

I try to match her speed.

"Noah? Where are you going?" the Guard's voice says in my helmet. "Is everything okay?"

I keep jabbing the air with my palm, my disk moving faster and faster. To Phoe, I mentally say, "Can you make him Forget he saw me?"

"Not a good idea," she says. "Making a single Guard Forget can easily put us on the Envoy's radar, and given that he already messaged his fellow Guards, I'd have to make all of them Forget, increasing the risk."

She takes a sudden left, and I follow, mentally shouting, "So I just try to outrun them?"

"That's the best course of action, yes. They don't know who you really are. They think one of their own is acting funny. If we lose them, it'll never get back to you. Once we finish the Test, I might be able to make them Forget in a way that would not alert the Envoy—" Her words cut off, and then she whispers, "Shit. They're already here."

Two Guards are in front of us, the fiery display reflecting off their astronaut helmets.

We turn so suddenly I feel lucky the food I ate in the man cave was virtual. Otherwise, it might've joined my heart in my throat.

Phoe is going at least fifty miles per hour as she whooshes ahead. I follow her, going nearly as fast, but to my dismay, she mentally shouts, "They're gaining on us. Watch out!"

If she hadn't warned me, my pursuers might've had to peel me off the metal surface of the cone-shaped building. The side of my disk scrapes the sharp metal tip of the structure, sending sparks flying, and my disk shakes violently. In a miraculous feat of agility, I manage not to fall off the disk.

"If by 'miraculous' you mean I took control of your hand just in time, then sure," Phoe says. "Watch for that one."

I duck instinctively before I realize why.

A white-gloved hand slides over my helmet.

"Instinctively, sure," Phoe murmurs in my ear. "Nothing to do with me."

"Don't distract me by taking credit for everything," I think back. "Wait, why are you going up so sharply?"

Before I get the chance to hesitate, my palm points up, and I do a swift reaching motion, as if I'm trying to grab something before someone can steal it from me. I'm not sure if this movement was mine or Phoe's influence, but I do know that it caused the disk to torpedo up so fast that I can't help but close my eyes in horror. When I open them, I see Phoe's disk in front of me, zigzagging madly. I realize my disk is doing the same and fight the urge to close my eyes again.

"Noah, stop, what are you doing?" a voice says over the helmet's radio.

If my pursuers are concerned about my maneuvers, I figure I should be worrying three times as much. To distract myself from the dread gathering in my stomach, I ask, "Phoe, how do they know I'm this Noah guy? All the outfits are the same."

She clicks her fingers and says, "Look at the other Guards."

I do and see little nametag-like labels show up on the interface of my visor for each Guard.

"You each have a unique radio identification in these helmets," Phoe explains.

I glance back again and reflect on the fact that the Guards are clustering. It's odd that they're *not* closing in on me. They're acting as though something is giving them pause.

Something bright and loud explodes next to my right shoulder.

I'm nearly blinded by the sudden flash of red fire. Then there's a green explosion, followed by a yellow one. Did the Guards shoot a bunch of rockets at me?

Then I understand. These are rockets of a different sort; they're the Birth Day fireworks. To punctuate my realization, another piece of artillery explodes about a foot away from the bottom of my disk. Another one hits the disk, the impact nearly pushing me off.

"Phoe, you flew us directly into the fireworks? Are you insane?"

A new explosion erupts two feet above my head, and a rain of small firefly-like embers descends. The few specks of fire that land on my helmet and shoulders go out without causing any damage.

"That isn't so surprising, given that you're wearing a space suit. Even in ancient times, those things were fireproof. What's important is that I got us away from them." Phoe looks back.

I follow her gaze.

She's right. The Guards aren't suicidal enough to chase after us—fireproof suits or not. As I watch, they disperse, flying in all directions.

"Crap, I think they're trying to form a sphere around us, like they did before. If we let them, they'll tighten the perimeter after the fireworks are done. Let's not let that happen." Phoe guides her disk right next to mine and tilts her hand downward, almost at a ninety-degree angle.

She plummets.

My lungs seize. "Phoe, I can't do that," I think at her frantically. "There are projectiles flying at us, not to mention—"

I stop speaking because, for the first time, I truly feel Phoe's influence on my hand. Nothing else would explain its current position, with the tips of my fingers pointing at my toes.

My disk plunges toward the ground. A firework is flying toward my face. I swerve, unwilling to learn how impact-proof the helmet is. The rocket misses the visor and explodes with a violent roar.

"Noah, stop. You will get yourself killed," a voice says over the helmet's radio. My fellow Guards must be watching my current descent.

For all its insanity, Phoe's desperate idea has one payoff: there aren't any Guards in our path. They failed to corner me.

"They failed so far," Phoe corrects. "We're turning toward the Elderly section. The Barrier should hide us from them for a few crucial moments."

This time, it feels like it was me who changed the direction of my flight, but it could easily be my brain confabulating this choice. Whatever the cause, I turn my palm parallel to the ground. The disk mirrors the movement, and instead of falling, I'm now racing forward.

In the distance, Guards are flying down like gigantic bits of hail. The sky is teeming with them. The fireworks enhance the feeling of us being surrounded by some kind of surreal force of nature.

I don't slow down.

A Guard flies directly into my path, in the spot where Phoe's virtual form just passed.

"Faster," Phoe yells, and my hand juts forward.

The Guard races faster toward me too.

This is again like that game of chicken the ancients liked to play, only in the air instead of on a flat surface with a car. I bet even *they* would consider what I'm doing crazy.

The rational part of me knows that Phoe must have calculated this maneuver with her super-duper AI mathematical skills, and that despite what the lizard part of my brain thinks, I won't crash into this Guard and die. Still, I swear the black underside of the Guard's disk—or at least the shiny metal edge—is about to hit my helmet.

Except it doesn't.

All I feel is a bit of turbulence as the Guard zooms right past me. Thanking the laws of aerodynamics for keeping me alive so far, I project my palm forward with such force that my shoulder joint pops. It's unclear whether I did that maneuver because Phoe made me or as a nervous tick.

As I continue rocketing forward, beads of sweat drip into my eyes, and the helmet prevents me from clearing them.

"On it," Phoe says, and a warm puff of air makes the moisture go away.

As my vision clears, I see the Barrier shimmering in the distance. It's reflecting the northern lights and the fireworks, and we're soaring right for it.

"Don't look up," Phoe says in my mind.

The surest way to have someone look up is by telling them not to.

I look up and regret not following Phoe's advice. Three Guards are overhead and flying downward, like hawks zeroing in on yummy, fluffy prey.

It sucks that I'm cast in the role of that prey.

Phoe abandons all pretense of giving me free will. My arm tilts sideways, and my disk instantly does the same. It's a marvel I don't fall off it.

"Your boots attach you to the disk with a powerful magnet," Phoe says sharply. "That's the case with all Guards. How do you think they stay on at those angles?"

I don't think. I'm too preoccupied with trying not to have a heart attack. I'm doing the disk equivalent of a somersault, over and over.

"Actually, I think the official term for this maneuver is *salto mortale*," Phoe says helpfully.

I don't chide her for being a smartass. That's how scared I am. If the ancient game of football involved people trying to tackle you from the sky, this is what it would look like.

Every time one of them misses me, they join the others in pursuit behind me. I have about forty of them on my tail when I plunge into the Barrier—with another somersault.

When we appear on the Elderly side of the Barrier, my heart sinks, and that's a feat considering it was already at my feet.

In front of me is an impenetrable wall of Guards.

CHAPTER SIXTEEN

"It's worse than you think," Phoe whispers. "It's not a wall. It's a half-sphere. There are Guards above and below. And before you suggest we head back, they're doing the same thing on the other side."

I scan the scene and confirm Phoe's words. We're surrounded, and the Guards in front of us are readying their Stun Sticks.

"You might want to close your eyes," Phoe says. "I'm about to try something that's a little more extreme."

As tempting as it is, I don't dare close my eyes. She's never labeled any of her crazy stunts 'extreme' before.

The Guards move toward me. The helmet's radio comes alive, and a soothing voice says, "Relax, Noah. You're having some kind of episode. We're trying to help—"

I don't hear the rest because Phoe begins her 'extreme' moves. Or more accurately, I execute the moves Phoe wants me to make—moves so insane they leave no doubt about who's in charge of my body.

The first maneuver starts innocuously enough. I touch my right fingers together.

"That undoes the magnetic pull of the disk," Phoe explains.

Then the insanity starts. Squatting on the disk, I grab its edge and give it a violent pull. I fall instantly, clutching the disk against my chest like a medieval shield.

If it isn't clear, I fall because there's no longer a disk under my feet.

As I'm plummeting toward the Guards below me, time slows. I have a chance to reflect on Phoe's plan, or the lack of it. Is she hoping the Guards, fearing the impact, will allow me to keep falling to my death, or is she hoping I won't break my legs on the Guards' helmets if they don't move?

In a spinning wrist-wrenching motion, I throw the disk under my feet. The magnets do their job, and I'm once again attached to the disk. The disk comes alive and slows my frantic descent. The Guards below me don't fly apart as I thought they might, and I'm two feet above their heads.

I grab the disk by the edge again and land on their slippery helmets. The slowing maneuver I executed makes this landing only mildly uncomfortable. As soon as I can, I run across people's shoulders and heads, dodging their Stun Sticks.

My speed increases as I run forward. I think I understand Phoe's plan. The Guards aren't forming a perfect half-sphere. There are Guards on the bottom and Guards to the side, but the place where they meet is a weak point. One Guard recognizes our plan and hurries to get in my way. I keep running across the Guards, dodging their hands and Sticks as I go. The clever Guard flies at me on his disk.

When the collision seems inevitable, I nearly close my eyes. My body twists at the last moment, and I swing the disk at his legs like a blunt weapon.

The disk connects with a hard thwack, and the Guard swerves, clutching his legs. Getting hit on the shin with a metal disk must really hurt.

His trajectory takes him into the swirling mass of Guards below. In a continuous motion, I lower the disk in my hands and jump onto it. My feet attach, and my arm jolts forward, granting me speed. I whoosh through the sliver of space that separates the top and bottom Guards, just as Phoe probably planned.

"By the time the Guards regroup, we'll have a few precious seconds of a lead," Phoe says after she appears next to me, standing on her illusory disk.

Only now do I realize she was missing for the last few seconds.

"I focused extra attention on keeping you alive," she explains. "Looks like we might actually reach our target. Do you remember that black building?" Phoe waves northeast.

"Yes, we passed by it the other day," I subvocalize.

"That's where the Test is taking place," she says. "We shouldn't go there directly. You see that building?" She points slightly left. A tall, tetrahedron-shaped silver building towers over the landscape. "That's where we're heading."

My arm lurches in that direction, as does the disk. When I think I can't go any faster, Phoe forces me to increase the speed again. Before I can have a heart attack, she increases the speed some more.

Everything goes quiet, and I wonder if we've reached the speed of sound.

"No, we're not going that fast. If we were, we'd be able to cross Oasis, side to side, twenty-five times in a second," Phoe says as a thought in my head. "We're travelling at a measly two hundred miles per hour."

I suspect she's being pedantic as a way of distracting me from my terror. It doesn't work. The view of the ever-approaching tetrahedron is all I can focus on.

"Close your eyes," Phoe says urgently.

Refusing to take the coward's way out, I keep my eyes open. The building gets closer and closer. We're not slowing down or changing course. It looks as though we're heading for a large window near the top floor.

The building is a few feet away.

The disk is slowing down, but not fast enough.

I try to tilt my hand, but it doesn't listen to me. Instead, I cover my head with my arms as we crash into the window. Shards of glass fly all around me, the sound deafening.

Before I can so much as gasp, I crash into the opposite wall, and the wind gets knocked out of me. Dazed, I notice broken clay all around me. Am I in some kind of arts-and-crafts studio?

My head is spinning, but I don't get a chance to catch my breath. Glass crunches under my feet as I jump up and gesture at the nearby door. As the door swings open, I notice a shriveled Elderly woman cowering in the corner of the room.

"She's not hurt, just frightened," Phoe explains as she makes my legs rush me out of the room and toward the emergency staircase. "We need to run down and make our way to that black structure."

My feet pound the floor to the rhythm of my frenzied heartbeat as I descend the staircase. Phoe's worried form appears in front of me. She's looking over my shoulder.

As I turn to follow her gaze, my visor goes into the blue-and-red heat vision mode she showed me earlier, and I see red shapes running up the stairs.

"Guards. They're on their way up here," Phoe hisses. I automatically look up, and she frantically shakes her head. "We can't go back."

She's right. There are more red blobs coming down than going up. I look sideways and see another red shape in one of the rooms. The shape is heading for the exit.

"Is it one of the Guards?" I subvocalize so frantically I nearly say the words out loud. "Did they jump in through a window?"

"I don't think so," Phoe says, following my gaze. "Go there and prepare your Stun Stick."

I head back up the stairs to the landing, and from there, I enter the building's forty-fifth floor. I make my way to the door where the figure is moving.

The red body heat outline looks like it's making a gesture. The door begins to slide open. If there's a Guard behind it after all, I just walked into his clutches.

I ready the Stun Stick and say, "Phoe, how do I turn off the heat vision?"

My vision returns to normal just as the door opens.

I raise my arm to stun the person who's coming out but stop cold. It's not a person—well, obviously, it's a person, but he or she is wearing the weirdest costume I've ever seen.

A plush purple creature is standing at the threshold. It looks like a cross between a dragon and a hippopotamus. The hippo-dragon's face is frozen in an overfriendly smile, and its short arms cover a green underbelly.

"Can I help you?" the hippo-dragon asks in a hoarse masculine voice.

"Will stunning him work through that contraption?" I think at Phoe with as much urgency as one can put in a thought.

"It should—it works through these suits, though I guess they're more conductive. Tell him to take the head off," she urges. "I turned off the radio in your helmet so the Guards won't hear this exchange."

"Please take off your head," I say, giving my voice the arrogant air of authority I associate with the Guards.

"The helmet already disguises your voice," Phoe whispers. "But that was a nice touch."

The man raises his hands to his head and pulls the smiling headgear up.

As soon as I see a sliver of neck between the purple cloth, I touch the Stun Stick to it and press the button.

The purple monster falls down, the grinning head rolling to the side. The Elderly man underneath must be one of the younger members. His hair is only beginning to gray.

"Move him inside and take that outfit off him," Phoe orders. "We don't have much time."

I drag my victim inside his room. The room is filled with crocheting paraphernalia and has an odd, musty smell. I drag the man out of the purple outfit.

"Should I swap clothes with him?" I ask Phoe.

Underneath the bright colors, the man is wearing a drab gray outfit that reminds me of what Youths typically wear.

"No, just put the dinosaur suit on." A whisper of mirth enters her voice. "You should be able to wear it on top of your Guard getup."

"What the hell? Why was an Elderly dressed like this?" I step into the bottom portion of the purple costume and pull it up over my Guard suit, finding it a surprisingly loose fit. I reach down to pick up the head of the monster and ask, "And how do you know it's a dinosaur and not a dragon or a hippo?"

"It's his Birth Day masquerade outfit," Phoe says. "They're all wearing them outside. I think this person works with little kids, and they probably get a kick out of this costume. And I know it's a dinosaur because I'm fairly sure this is Barney—a Tyrannosaurs Rex ancient kids used to watch on TV. I'll get you an episode from the archives one day. For now, please, we need to hurry."

I put on the dinosaur head, mumbling about ancients and their obsession with violence. Using a T-Rex as entertainment for little ones? Granted, they did make him look warm and fuzzy.

Clumsily exiting the apartment, I head for the stairs. With the head on, I see the world through two small pinholes. I can't picture walking down the stairs this way, but—

"No, the Guards are on the stairs. We'll take the elevator. This way." Phoe walks down the corridor. "Come on, stalk me, you monster."

Ignoring her mockery, I reach the elevator and do the summoning gesture. Given the small arms of T-Rexes and the suit based on their anatomy, my gesture comes out clumsy. Still, the elevator arrives in an instant.

"I summoned the elevator." Phoe snickers and walks in. "Can you move your tail?"

With the tail trailing behind me, I stomp into the elevator and cross my arms around my green chest. Seeing her chuckle again, I think angrily, "Can you make this thing go down, or are we waiting for the Guards to catch up with us?"

Not waiting for her to comply, I press the manual button but have trouble because the purple plush arm of my costume only has two giant fingers.

The elevator closes, and Phoe belly-laughs at my discomfort. However, as we get closer to the ground floor, she turns more serious, and by the time the doors open, her face is a mask of concentration.

Two Guards are standing there, their helmeted heads tilted in a way that tells me they're looking inside the elevator.

CHAPTER SEVENTEEN

My blood pressure spiking, I wave my two-fingered paw at them and lumber out of the elevator like I own the building.

I fully expect them to ask me to take the head off, but they don't. Instead, as I head down the corridor, one of the Guards says, "Have fun out there."

I repeat the moronic hand wave and follow Phoe as she walks out of the lobby.

Though the suit severely restricts my movements, I'm glad for the anonymity it provides. Guards are surrounding the building, but they pay the dinosaur no attention.

Phoe heads toward the black building, and I walk after her, trying not to gawk at the dressed-up Elderly all around me. Phoe was right. The best explanation for their funky costumes is that this is some kind of masquerade. We pass by Pinocchio, a red M&M candy, and a huge crowd of ancient rulers that include the King of Spades, the Lion King, and Barack Obama.

Despite my anxiety, I can't help but envy the Elderly. The Youths never get to dress up like this, not even on Birth Day.

"This is so they can take the new generation of little kids outside for Birth Day without the kids seeing any signs of aging. Also, if it makes you feel any better, I believe the Elderly are thinking about doing something like this for the Youths next year. They're testing this out on themselves this year, perhaps to see whether it will corrupt the Youths." Phoe shakes her head. "I guess they discovered the one holiday Birth Day didn't already copycat—Halloween."

"I hope you're right about next year," I think, staring at a man dressed as Bugs Bunny. "Liam would love this."

"Sorry to cut this short, but that's our destination." She nods at the black building—or rather, a building made of metal that has a black sheen to it.

"Do I just walk in wearing this costume?" I think at Phoe.

"Yes, wear it, and if anyone sees you, pretend to have randomly wandered in from the street," she says.

"Okay." I head for the door, but she steps in front of me, a worried expression on her face. I instantly stop. "What is it, Phoe?"

"After you walk in, I won't be able to talk to you freely," she says, shifting from foot to foot. "This building is worse than the Witch Prison. I only happen to know the location of the Test room from the instructional message the eligible Test takers received earlier today."

She gestures, and a map overlay shows up on the Screen inside my visor.

"As you can see, all you need to do is walk down two corridors and turn left. Once you're there, there should be an obvious way to start the Test by placing your palm on the control panel. Whisper, 'Glove off,' to your helmet, and it will come off, though I'm not sure skin contact is required. You can handle something like that on your own, right?"

"Won't I need you? Inside the Test, I mean?" I step back and nearly trip over my costume's purple tail.

"That's what the Pi Trojan is for," Phoe reminds me. "As soon as you're in the Test, it will give me a way in."

"What about walking my body out of here during the Test? Isn't that part of the plan?"

"Once I'm in the Test, I'm sure I can patch back into your body."

"I guess." I take an uncertain step forward.

"You can do this." Phoe leans toward me and kisses my silly outfit on the cheek. "Go before the Guards figure out you're not in that tetrahedron building."

The reminder about our pursuers finally leads me to act.

Taking in a deep breath, I quietly walk into the black building.

"Phoe?" I think as I cross the spacious entryway. "Can you really not hear me in here?"

She doesn't respond, so I follow the map in my visor.

I turn into the northeast corridor and manage to take two shuffling steps in before I can't continue any farther.

A Guard stands in my way.

"Can I help you?" the Guard asks, his voice gruff and unfriendly.

A number of things happen in quick succession. I let my right arm hang loose at my pudgy purple side, while underneath the suit, I pull my actual arm, still dressed in the Guard outfit, out of the purple cloth around it. I then reach for the Stun Stick in my belt and say, "Where am I? I have a hard time seeing in this outfit. Can you help me take this head off?"

The Guard shrugs and steps toward me.

I reach for the dinosaur head with my left hand and pretend to fumble. With my right hand, under the suit, I raise the Stun Stick up to my neck.

The Guard places his hands on my purple headgear and pulls.

As soon as there's an inch of space between the two pieces of the dinosaur's skin, I jab the Guard with the Stun Stick and spasmodically press the button.

The Guard collapses on the spot.

Blowing out a relieved breath, I take his Stun Stick, figuring two weapons are better than one. Then I take the rest of my purple suit off, rip the tail off, and use it to tie the Guard's arms behind his back. Not sure how well this will keep him bound, I also put the dinosaur headgear on his head, only backward. This way, he won't see where he is when he regains consciousness. Finally, I rip up the rest of the suit and tie strips around the Guard's legs and across his torso and shoulders. Happy with my work, I drag his limp body into a nook in the corridor and zap him one more time for good measure.

Free to move again, I run toward my destination.

The next two turns are uneventful, and the third one should be the last. According to my map, the Test is right there, in a spacious room.

I turn the corner.

The Test room is empty except for two things: a large, lit-up wall to my right, and the Guard turning my way to my left.

"Hello, Ronny," I say, taking advantage of his nametag label in my visor's interface. Before he can react, I move in to close the distance between us.

"Noah?" he says, his posture uncertain.

I get closer and fib, "I'm here to relieve you of your duties. It's a little happy Birth Day surprise."

I don't know if he's reaching for his Stun Stick because he heard over his radio about everyone chasing after 'Noah' or because my improvisation was completely out of character with what a sane Guard would say, but the fact remains: he's reaching for it. I'm four feet away, so we're both outside Stun Stick reach. This is when I realize I'm holding on to my extra Stun Stick, another reason Ronny might be paranoid.

I throw my extra weapon at his head. He raises his hands. If it's to catch the Stun Stick, he fails. If it's to protect his visor, he's being silly. This helmet can easily withstand that impact. I use his momentary distraction to punch his midsection.

He staggers back.

I pull out my second Stun Stick.

He manages to take his out.

As though looking in a mirror, we touch the other's shoulder with the sticks. It's a matter of whose finger will press the button first.

I squeeze mine just as my consciousness escapes.

* * *

I wake up as though from a horrible nightmare. Where am I? Why is my bed so uncomfortable?

Then reality reasserts itself. An unconscious Guard is lying at my feet. I'm in the Test room, and we just zapped each other. If I've regained consciousness, that means the Guard, Ronny, is about to come to as well. It also means the Guard I left behind—the one tied up with the dinosaur outfit—is awake and trying to free himself.

I sit up and reach for the Stun Stick to my right. In a flurry of movements, Ronny grabs my ankle and pulls. His other arm reaches for his own Stick. I kick at his helmet and roll right, grabbing the Stun Stick as I go. Jumping to my feet, I see him do the same.

We circle each other slowly.

He lunges with the Stick, aiming at my right shoulder. I jump to the side, his Stick missing me by a hair, and counter by bringing down my weapon on his wrist like the ancient club it resembles.

The brute-force maneuver works, and his Stun Stick clanks on the floor. He follows it with his eyes—a big mistake. Using his distraction, I touch his exposed torso and pump him full of volts.

He crashes to the ground.

Breathing heavily, I drag his body to the wall where the Test is. There's a pedestal with a large palm-shaped indentation. Phoe mentioned there would be something like this when she sent me in. I drag Ronny closer to the control panel and zap him again to give myself the maximum amount of time to take the Test.

I place my hand on the indentation.

Nothing happens.

"Glove off," I whisper, remembering Phoe's instruction.

The glove separates from the suit, and I put it under my belt. With a deep breath out, I place my naked palm on the control panel.

A giant Screen appears on top of the panel. On the Screen are the words: *Authenticating age.*

I swallow. Phoe's insane idea of making me ninety years old is about to get tested. After a moment, the Screen turns green—universal for confirmed—and a giant panel slides out of the wall. Upon closer inspection, I realize it's a bed.

Lie down, Test subject Theodore, the Screen states. *Once you're in a horizontal position, initiate sleep.*

I expected the world to go white, the way it does on my trips to Virtual Reality and the IRES game. I didn't expect to take a nap. There's no helping it, though. I drag poor Ronny under the bed, get on, and zap him one last time.

Then I lie down and tighten the muscles around my eyes to initiate assisted sleep.

CHAPTER EIGHTEEN

I'm standing in a tunnel made of shimmering, translucent material. It looks as though water is somehow staying upright, creating the walls of this place. The material even ripples like water. There is no sky. The water walls keep going up, seemingly indefinitely, blending into the horizon of the non-existent sky. There are also doors here, doors that look like they're made of ice. The row of doors stretches out in both directions as far as the eye can see.

"Theo?" Phoe's thought says in my mind.

"Yes," I mentally respond. "Looks like your Pi trick worked."

"Forget about that." Her thought is urgent. "We need to abort this Test."

"Why?" I subvocalize.

"Don't subvocalize." Her mental reply is uncharacteristically sharp. "Look like you're trying to choose a door."

I do as she says. Turning right, I walk down the tunnel, gazing from one identical door to the next.

"What's going on?" I think at her, trying to control my anxiety. "Why are you so spooked?"

"This is too risky. I thought the Test would involve Virtual Reality, not *this.*"

"What do you mean? How can this not be VR? Are you saying this is the real world?" I look at the water walls and the lack of sky. "This environment is clearly fake."

"Okay, I don't want to split hairs about terminology. You could call it a Virtual Reality of sorts, but what makes it different is *you.* Specifically, how your mind arrived here." Phoe's thoughts hold an undertone of worry. "You see, Virtual Reality typically involves your neurons experiencing fake inputs and outputs from your nanos, a bit like Augmented Reality but taken to the extreme. It's your meat brain that goes through the experience. This place doesn't work like that." Her worry seems to intensify. "There's a feature in your nanos I noticed a while back. They seem to record what happens to your connectome, which is the combination of everything in your brain that makes up who you are, from your neurons to the lowliest neurotransmitter. I never realized how detailed that snapshot is or that it was used for any practical purpose in Oasis. I assumed it was dormant technology left over from your Singularity legacy. That the Elderly use this technology is hypocritical, but in hindsight, given Forgetting and all that, I don't know why I'm surprised."

"Hold on." I stop her from going off on her 'the Elderly hate technology and they're hypocrites' tangent. "I'm not sure I follow, Phoe. What are you saying?"

"Have you ever heard of uploading people? Did they scare you with such a concept at the Institute?"

I strain to recall such a term. "No."

"Okay, imagine if someone took a person, scanned them with nanotechnology, and created a perfect replica of them inside a simulated environment. This copy would be indistinguishable from the original, at least insofar as when you talk to them or how they feel about themselves."

"Kind of like the way you work? Your body that talks to me, that is?" I feel ice forming at the bottom of my chest. "Like what you said in the cave?"

"Kind of. My other self designed my body. It's not a copy of someone else's. But the principle of it, running emulated neurons and the rest, is the same. The mechanics of how an upload works is also similar to the way that version of my body does—"

"And you're saying that I'm—"

"—currently an upload," she says in my mind. "Your real brain is sleeping back on that bed."

I examine my clothes. I'm wearing an ancient outfit of dark jeans and a blue t-shirt, but that happens in regular VR. My thought process is the same. My emotions—particularly my overwhelming fear—feel realistic. The more I think about being this disembodied digital echo of myself, the less it makes sense. I feel normal. I'm here, breathing air and having a mental conversation with Phoe.

Okay, so I feel like my version of normal.

"I don't want to start philosophizing," Phoe responds, "but you wouldn't feel a difference, since the emulation the Test created is perfect. You are you in every sense of the word, except that on a very small scale, I doubt this place emulates the molecules that make you up. Then again, some of your 'real' body's molecules change from day to day and get replaced with new ones at varying rates. So yeah, being an upload doesn't make you any less real. That's part of the problem."

"Fine, so I'm an upload," I think tersely. "It's not what you expected to happen, I get that, but what's the difference? What's the danger you're so concerned about?"

"I don't even know where to begin." Phoe's thoughts enter my mind faster. "For starters, your brain's state is easier to manipulate here. The Test can make you forget or misremember things, whereas VR can't. I'm not sure how much I can protect you from that. What worries me more is that anything that happens to you here will get written back into your real-world brain by the Test's interface at the very end, before you wake up in the real world. If, say, you get so scared you develop a permanent stutter, your real brain will also get damaged and you'll develop a stutter, potentially for a long time, if not for the rest of your life."

"That isn't how the IRES game operates? I'm fairly sure I developed a fear of insects after that fight with a giant mechanical scorpion."

"No. Fear of bugs is a natural human response, and when you saw them, you merely learned something about yourself. Your core self wasn't changed by it. If you hit your head and wake up with amnesia in IRES, after the game is over, you'll be back to normal. This Test is different. If you develop amnesia and come back to your body before your memory is restored, the loss will be permanent. But that's not even the most frightening difference between the Test and IRES. If you die here, this version of you will really be dead. The Test doesn't make any backups of you or anything like that. If you die, you'll wake up in your body, and it will be as though this conversation never happened. Death means no information is written back to your sleeping self. Even if you lived in this place for thirty years, longer than you've been alive outside, those years would be gone. That person you became would be gone."

"But I would still wake up out there." Despite my words, I feel a growing anxiety. "Wouldn't it be more like a form of amnesia?"

"In my opinion, irreversible amnesia is a type of death. Imagine if in two seconds from now, something happened and you became a different person. Say you decided to dedicate your life to a noble cause, found love, or even became evil. All that would get erased if you—"

"But there's still that sleeping me," I think stubbornly. "How can you say I'd be dead?"

"I guess we have a different way of looking at existence. To me, we are, at the core, patterns of information. You're now a new pattern—a pattern that has seen these watery walls and diverged from the sleeping version of you. Until and unless your memories are written back, you're a new Theo. If you die, that will be final, and I don't know if I would consider the sleeping Theo the same person as you. He's still someone I care about, as are you, but you're two different people, until he remembers being you." She pauses. "Still, if your view of the matter makes you less scared, I'm glad. I would be petrified if I were you. I'd want to leave this place as soon as I could, and I insist we do just that."

"Okay," I think and stop next to another icy-looking door. "How do I escape?"

"I think if you walk without opening any doors or sit here looking dumb, the Test will eventually spit you out with a score of zero. I think that's your best course of action."

"But if I leave, doesn't that mean you won't get the resources we need?" I wipe my too-sweaty-considering-they-are-virtual palms on my shirt. "And doesn't that mean there's a good chance I'll be killed in the real world once Jeremiah gets the Council to vote on my neural scan?"

"I won't let that happen." Phoe's thought is like a lash in my brain.

"I know you would try to protect me," I think back. "But how can you protect me without messing with Jeremiah's mind? And what if the Envoy stops you or learns about you? We still don't know what he is and if he can kill you."

"I don't think I can be killed—not without destroying the ship. The worst the Envoy can do to me is lobotomize me again by taking away the resources I've gathered."

"Wouldn't that make you Forget so many things? Like our friendship?" She doesn't respond, so I press on. "Wouldn't that make this version of you die? Wouldn't that make the danger I'm currently facing pale in comparison?"

"My survival is more nuanced than yours, and I'm willing to take certain risks for your sake. For what it's worth, I took precautions by storing my important memories in a bunch of places, including the DMZ—"

I take a determined step toward the nearest door. That she would Forget that we kissed, or one of our many conversations, is unthinkable.

"I see what you're planning to do, Theo, and I beg you not to do it."

"Then you know how determined I am to keep *you* safe." I make my thoughts resolute. "I'm walking through this door, so please, just help me shut the Test down."

"No, Theo, that's another thing." Phoe sounds like she's on the verge of crying. "If this were VR, I would be limitless. But I don't have a real foothold in this world. I'm bound by the resources the Test allocated to you, which means there aren't any resources left for any type of sophisticated hacking. And, as I feared, there's an anti-intrusion algorithm running around this place. If it suspects my presence or doubts your integrity—"

I can tell she's just trying to convince me to leave, so I think, "You'll have to figure it out. I'm walking through this door." I take another step forward.

"Wait," Phoe hisses. "I have an idea."

I stop. "I thought you might. The least you can do is be completely honest with me."

"Fine. Beings that were near or exactly at human-level intelligence made this place, which means it's pretty buggy as far as software artifices go. I think I see a vulnerability already. Someone used a relatively small memory allocation to permanently store the Test score of every participant after it's sent out into the real world. In the right hands—my hands—that design choice could become this system's downfall."

"Phoe, if you're expecting a Eureka moment from me, it's clearly not happening," I think in frustration. "Break it down for me as though I have 'near-human-level' intelligence."

"The designer thought the scores would never go above a certain number. He knew many people will take the Test, so he was stingy on this memory space. That means that if you were to get a ridiculously high score on your Test, a condition called a buffer overrun will happen. It's when the system tries to cram a too-big value into a too-small-for-it space. I could exploit that to bring this whole system crashing down."

"So I'll just take the Test until I get the score you need," I think. "That sounds like a decent-enough plan."

"Yes, except this place will throw you out after you fail a predetermined number of times, which is most likely a single failure. Otherwise, everyone would have a super-high score."

"Can we cheat?" I absentmindedly touch one of the water walls. It feels like that Jell-O stuff Phoe told me about. "Can you figure out how I can reach a high score?"

"I can try," she responds. "But like I said, it's—"

"Blah, blah, too dangerous," I think with false bravado. "We settled this already. I'm doing this."

"In that case, I'll try to help you cheat," Phoe thinks grimly. "Obviously."

"Good. Now how long will this take? There's a Guard in the real world who may wake up from his zap-nap soon."

"I'm already in your mind, so yeah, I can get you out of the building. But there's something else you should know—another thing that makes this place a little different. You see, digital minds—like ours are right now—don't work as slowly as chemically bound meat ones. Your thought processes inside the Test are many times faster than in the real world. In other words, you may get a lot of Testing done in subjective, real-world time. That may be why someone opted to use this technology over VR."

"Time is running differently for me?" I can't help but feel a sense of wonder at that. "Kind of like it does for you?"

"Not at the same rate and without the massive parallelism I leverage, but it's a good comparison."

"Okay, that's good news. I have more time here." I brush my fingers against the door. As you'd expect from something made of ice, it feels extremely cold, almost burningly cold. "You should still get the sleeping version of me out of that room."

"Obviously," Phoe responds. "And before you ask, here. You can see the outside world through that." A familiar watch-Screen appears on my wrist. "The anti-intrusion stuff shouldn't notice anything that's on your body. The Test didn't make your clothes, but pulled them from your memories. You could've easily ended up with that watch on your own."

I look at the watch and see my real-world, Guard-disguised self lying unconscious, with the Guard also passed out near the bed.

"He, I mean you, I mean—let's call him Guard-Theo—is getting up already," Phoe says. "Due to the time differences, Guard-Theo's head is moving very slowly off the pillow. I wouldn't worry too much about the outside world if I were you. I only gave you that watch to keep you informed. I'll take care of your real body while you focus on taking the Test."

"Got it," I think but can't help glancing at the watch again. Nothing's changed. Time really is moving faster here.

"Good luck." Phoe's thought is imbued with trepidation. "I wish I could kiss you."

Without responding to her sentiment, I push on the icy door.

The door swings open, like in ancient times.

I walk through, and as soon as my whole body crosses the threshold, all my senses turn off.

CHAPTER NINETEEN

My mind is muddy. I can't recall how I got here. I'm even less sure where 'here' is. I'm standing by train tracks. Something about this doesn't make sense. I feel as though this is the first time I've ever seen train tracks, but I'm meant to treat them as a regular occurrence. Then again, if I never saw train tracks before, how do I know what they are?

"You're missing more than just those basics," a voice says. "I bet you don't even remember your name."

I look around. The voice was female, but I don't see any women in my immediate vicinity.

It occurs to me that the voice might be a thought in my mind, even if it was female. Worst of all, she might be right. I can't recall my name or much else for that matter. The oddest thing is that something is preventing me from panicking.

I hear screams in the distance. I run toward the sound to see what's going on.

The ground begins to shake.

I keep running until I crest a small hill. The tracks separate into a fork, one set of parallel metal lines becoming two. There's a large switch—a mechanical contraption designed to direct the train either left or right. Everything is set up to make a passing train go left. If someone needed to divert the train right, they would have to pull the red mechanical handle of the switch.

"For someone who's never seen train tracks, you sure know a lot about them," the mysterious female voice intrudes as a thought. "Strange, isn't it?"

I fleetingly question my sanity, but then I get distracted when I see the source of the screams.

Five people are tied to the tracks on the left. They're screaming their lungs out. Their terrified eyes are looking behind me.

The ground shakes with increasing violence, and a loud *tadum-tadum* sound is coming up somewhere behind me.

Before I get a chance to look back, I see another person tied to the tracks—on the right set. This person isn't screaming, but he looks distraught.

The noise gets overwhelming, and I finally look behind me.

I should've guessed.

It's a train barreling down the tracks with ever-increasing speed.

Belatedly, I understand why the five people are screaming. They're about to get killed. I look at them, then look back at the train. Then I look at the switch next to me.

I only have a moment to act.

My decision isn't rational. It's instinctive.

I pull the lever to save the five people, cognizant that I just doomed the man on the right.

The train whooshes past me and veers onto the right tracks. Before I witness the horrible result, my mind turns off.

* * *

I'm back in the Test corridor, surrounded by the water walls.

My name is Theo. Of course it is. How the hell did the Test make me forget something so basic?

"I told you," Phoe says in my head. "The Test messes with your mind."

"Fuck." I rub my temples. "This Test is wacky."

"Yeah." If it were possible to think disapprovingly, that's what Phoe's mental acknowledgment managed to do.

"But why?" I risk saying this out loud. I figure a normal person might say something like that to himself after living through that episode.

"To figure out your moral reasoning," Phoe thinks with that same undertone of distaste. "At least I guess that's the point. The scenario you saw is ancient. It's called the Trolley Problem."

"How did I do?"

"I think you made the Test makers happy," she replies. "Look at the door."

The door is no longer made of clear ice. It's now a solid piece of green gemstone, either malachite or quartz.

"Green for pass," Phoe explains. Then, dripping with sarcasm, she adds, "Great job."

"Why do I have a feeling you disapprove of something?" I think at her.

"It's not you," Phoe responds. "I can just see what's coming and what they want you to do to get a good score. Don't worry about my feelings. Just take the next Test. I'll try to make it so you're not as clueless about your identity as you were in the first one, or at the very least, I'll make sure when I talk to you, you can remember who I am."

"Sounds like a plan," I think and walk to the door next to the green one. "Wish me luck."

She doesn't say anything, so I walk through the doorway and my thoughts stop again, as if a light switch has gone off.

* * *

I'm standing in the middle of a plateau. Giant mountains surround me, their orange and red colors contrasting with the lapis lazuli of the midday sky. A sliver of metallic train tracks crosses through the rocks below. Someone's cut into the ancient mountainside to make way for human transportation.

My heart rate skyrockets. Despite my fuzzy memory, I know I'm absolutely terrified of heights.

A man is here. Correction, he might be a giant. He's so tall and broad-shouldered that I wonder if he isn't a statue carved into the rock face. But no, he's moving from one bare foot to another, proving his realness. He clearly doesn't like something he's looking at, because his tree-sized arms are tense and his hands are squeezed into fists.

Screams echo from below.

The screams are familiar, though I'm not sure where I heard them before.

I run up to the edge of the cliff farthest from the big guy. I have to swallow my heart back into my ribcage before I look down to see the source of the noise.

Right below, train tracks cross through a narrow passageway.

Five people are tied to these tracks, and, understandably, they're screaming.

Then I hear the honk and feel the vibrations of the oncoming train.

I instantly assess the situation.

The big guy is standing on a cliff between the screaming people and the train. There are only moments left before the train reaches them.

Conviction overcomes me. I don't know how, but I know with absolute certainty that this guy is so large that if he were to fall on those tracks, the train would halt and the five people would be saved. Someone of my size would get run over, though, and the train would keep going and kill the five people.

I also know there isn't enough time to ask the big man to sacrifice himself, and I'm sure the idea hasn't occurred to him.

My choices are clear.

I could run up to him and, before he realizes I'm here, push him down and save the people below. Alternatively, I could do nothing.

I freeze, appalled that the idea of pushing the man even entered my mind. Pushing him would be wrong. He's just standing here, watching this horrific event unravel. If I push him, my action will bring the horror onto him.

"Push him," Phoe thinks forcefully. "Quickly."

I know Phoe is a voice I should obey. I run toward the big man. My past rushes into my mind. I remember who Phoe is, who *I* am, and most importantly, I remember what I'm doing here.

The man stands there as I close the distance between us.

I slam into him. He falls down the cliff as though he really were carved out of rock. The train screeches below, but before I can see the consequences of my actions, my consciousness fades again.

* * *

I'm back in the never-ending hallway, surrounded by ice doors, though now there are two green gemstone ones among them.

"Do you see now?" Phoe thinks with agitation.

I suck in a breath, the horrifying images still fresh in my mind. "Why did you tell me to push that guy? I know this isn't real, but that wasn't the right thing to do. That wasn't—"

"Don't you understand? As far as the designers of this Test are concerned, that was the same exact choice as your first session. You had five people versus one in both cases. You could've done nothing in both cases. You ended up killing one person to save many, which is clearly what you should continue to do to get the best score. I'll try not to puke along the way."

She's right about the numbers, but something feels different about the two scenarios. Pushing someone to his death seems wrong, but flipping a switch to save a greater number of people doesn't.

Phoe mentally snorts. "This is why I'll never rely on human moral judgment when it comes to my survival. Just do the next one. I have a feeling the moral dilemmas get worse from here."

I walk up to the door on the right of the one I just passed. Before entering the room, I glance at my tiny Screen watch. During the Tests, I wasn't even aware that it was on my wrist.

Guard-Theo has barely lifted his helmeted head from the pillow.

"Wow, Phoe. You weren't kidding. Time is really messed up between these two places."

"Yeah, well, to get the buffer overrun, we'll be here for a while, so you'll be long out of that black building by the time we're through with the Test."

Shaking my head in confusion, I pass through the icy door, and predictably, the world goes away once more.

* * *

This time, the scenario is so odd I can't help but remember more about who I am—thanks to Phoe's meddling, of course. I'm Theo the Youth, not Theodore the surgeon, which is what the Test wants me to believe.

I'm in a room with five patients of 'mine.' I 'recall' that each patient is missing a vital organ. They each have only a day left to live. The reason they're all in the same room is that they have the same blood type, meaning that if an organ comes in from a person who's a match for any of these guys, it can be brought into this room for expediency.

"This isn't scientifically, medically, or even historically accurate," Phoe thinks, but I ignore her, curious where this is going.

I exit the room because I recall I need to make my rounds. I walk down the corridor, determined to check on a patient recovering from a minor surgery. I look at his chart. He came to get his tonsils removed, but he's now ready to check out, pending my sign-off. Then something catches my eye. He has the same blood type as the five unfortunate patients. Were he to donate his organs, those five people would live. Of course, he wouldn't do this of his own volition. Without those five vital organs, he would die.

The question for me, as the surgeon who can save those lives, is—

"No," I think at Phoe. "The Test creators can't mean this."

"In terms of sheer numbers, it's the same Trolley problem: five versus one," Phoe thinks. "We know what you have to do to get a good score."

“I’m not killing this innocent person so I can harvest his organs.” Everything inside me rebels at the notion. “I won’t do it. It’s not just morally wrong—it’s sick and disgusting.”

“This is not real, remember? This is just a Test.”

I point at the donor guy. “Except for the cutting him up bit. Even though I know it’s not real, I don’t think I can do it.”

“I can make it so you’re not aware you’re doing it,” Phoe says mentally. “But it’s risky.”

“Why don’t I forfeit this specific scenario and pass some other one?” I think at her, placing the guy’s chart back at the foot of the bed.

“It might get harder from here. Keep in mind this was designed by people who thought it was morally justified to Forget Mason. To get the high score, either you need to fight your squeamishness, or we have to risk my solution.”

I picture doing what the Test requires and feel instant nausea at the whole idea. This is futile. If I can’t even imagine picking up a scalpel, how can I put it into someone’s body?

“Then let me take over, risk be damned,” Phoe thinks. “The idea is simple. I suppress your conscious thoughts and move your body around—not unlike what's happening in the outside world."

"And I won't see it? I won't be aware of what my body is doing?"

"No. It will be a gap in your memory, if that's the solution you choose."

I hesitate for a moment, then nod. "Fine. Let's try it with this scenario."

"Okay," Phoe replies.

My mind doesn't go blank, at least not in the way it does when I enter and exit these Test scenarios. It feels more like a gap in my recall, like when I first wake up. The grim task Phoe had to do is like a forgotten nightmare. I know it happened, because that's the best way to explain the situation I find myself in: I'm standing in a room with the five patients coming to their senses, their vitals normal.

Before I can register the horrifying fact that an innocent man is dead, the Test registers my score, and my brain short-circuits again.

CHAPTER TWENTY

I'm back in the corridor, next to three measly green doors. I shudder at the thought of what the next Test scenario will bring.

"How much longer do I have to do this?" I look at the multitude of remaining doors on both sides. "How high does my score have to be?"

"So high it's best you don't think about it," Phoe responds. "Let's focus on the positive: since the designers didn't expect anyone to get too high of a score, I suspect they didn't plan enough unique scenarios either. That means that at some point, these Tests will repeat themselves."

"Why can't someone else get a super-high score?" I wonder. "As disgusting as that last scenario was, the rule of 'always save the most people' isn't hard to figure out and mindlessly follow. I'm sure some Test takers did just that."

"I don't think you'll just face moral dilemmas here," Phoe says. "Just keep going and we'll see."

* * *

The next two scenarios are also moral dilemmas. They deal with a lifeboat and aren't as disgusting as the last scenario. After Phoe tells me what I have to do, I decide I can manage them myself. She claims these scenarios are also based on ancient moral dilemma classics, and I take her word for it.

The sixth scenario is something I recognize. It's called the Prisoner's Dilemma, and I choose 'cooperation' even before Phoe suggests that as the way to score the point.

When I enter the seventh door, things are a little different.

For one, I fully remember almost everything about myself, just not how I arrived here, in Instructor George's class.

No one else is here except the two of us. There are three strange-looking doors at the front of the room.

"Find the door that leads out of here, and you can skip the next three Lectures, Theodore," the Instructor says. "Go ahead, based on a hunch, which of these would you open? You can choose it now, but don't open it yet. I will give you an option to change your choice."

I point at the rightmost door.

"Here's the twist," Instructor George says. "I'm going to toss this coin." He shows me the ancient artifact as though it's the most natural thing for him to be holding. "If the coin lands on heads, I'll open the middle door and show you if it's your winning door. If so, you're obviously out of luck." He tosses the coin.

"It's tails," he announces while opening the leftmost door. Pointing at the red wall behind the door, he says, "This door is a losing choice, so it all comes down to this: Do you want to switch your choice from the rightmost door to the middle one? I will allow you to switch, if you so choose."

I look at the two doors. No one is getting killed this time, which is good, but I don't fully get the point of what's going on. It's a fifty-fifty proposition, and I might as well stick with the rightmost door, since I feel attached to it.

"No, Theo." Phoe's thought is disappointed. "Choose to switch."

"I want to switch," I tell Instructor George.

As suddenly as I utter those words, I return to the Test hallway.

The door I just went through is green, but I don't understand why.

"Because the logical thing to do was switch to the door with the higher chance of being the winner," Phoe explains.

"What are you talking about?" I object. "It was fifty-fifty either way."

"No, it was one out of three for your first choice, but two out of three in the case of that middle door."

I frown. "No, it wasn't."

"Trust me." Phoe's thought is amused. "It's called the Monty Hall Problem, and you're free to look it up in your leisure time, assuming such a thing will ever happen. Don't beat yourself up for not understanding it. It's famous for its counter-intuitiveness, and I suspect it's problems like these that answer your earlier question about high scores. Many people would've gotten this wrong, and the Test would've ended."

"Fine. I don't want to argue. I'm getting tired of this, and I want it over with."

"I'm sorry to break it to you, but it won't be over for a very, very long time." Phoe pauses, then thinks at me, "It's not too late to quit."

"No, we proceed as planned." I walk confidently toward the next door.

The scenario is a moral dilemma again. It's a twist on the first train situation I encountered. The single difference is that I remember living in the same house as the person I have to sacrifice. His name is John. This leads me to not want to flip the switch, but I do. In the next situation, it's the train scenario again, but instead of John—a stranger I theoretically knew—I have to sacrifice Liam. Flipping the switch on my own is too hard, so I ask Phoe to take over my body.

The next few scenarios, according to Phoe, come from an ancient IQ test. In every case, I mentally tell her what I want to do, and she tells me if I'm wrong so I don't fail the Test.

After what feels like hours, I gaze at the row of at least a hundred green doors. "Will I eventually get hungry or thirsty?" I ask Phoe.

"This place wasn't designed to give you a chance to do these Tests long enough to feel those urges," she responds. "In your special case, since I have access to the resources the Test allocated to emulate you, I can adjust things so you don't feel hunger or thirst. It's akin to how I was able to give you that watch."

I look at my hand. At this point in the real world, Theo has finally gotten his head off the pillow, and his feet are on the floor. In other words, a few seconds have passed in the real world, even though I've been taking this Test for ages.

"That is why I advise you against looking at the watch in the future," Phoe says. "In general, avoid any references to the passage of time. You're going to be stuck in this Test for so long that it's best you don't pay close attention to what's going on outside.

I can make you alert, but even I can't help you if you get fed up."

"No looking at the watch, check," I think and confidently walk to the next icy door.

This time, the logic-testing stuff merges with the moral dilemma scenarios. I'm presented doors, and opening them saves or kills people. After this, more of the previous Tests get mingled.

I take Test after Test for what feels like a week. Maybe it is a week. I don't know because I refuse to look at my watch, as Phoe suggested.

On the next iteration, I'm faced with the original Trolley problem: five people on one side, a single person on the other, and a switch.

"Looks like the Test has come full circle, like you predicted," I think.

"Yes," Phoe agrees tersely. "But—"

"Does this mean we're almost done?"

"I knew that would be your next question. No, we are far from getting a high-enough score for a buffer overrun. I'm sorry. What's worse is that I doubt I can convince you to quit."

"What makes you so sure?" I ask, knowing full well she's right.

"I could say it was your answers during the sunken costs scenario, but really, it's because I can read your stubborn mind."

Instead of responding, I walk to the next door. The scenario is the one where I have to push a guy off the cliff.

After I do the full Test circle a few more times, I realize a month, maybe even a few months, have gone by since I last looked at the watch-Screen.

I allow myself the guilty action and look. Guard-Theo is walking outside, with Guards following him.

"What happened?" I think at Phoe. "Are they trying to catch us again?"

"I had to run an errand on the side," Phoe explains. "They caught up with me afterwards. I'm about to have us jump on a disk. With your attitude toward heights, you might not want to look at the watch for a while."

"I could live the rest of my life and be happy if I never, ever have to fly again," I think at her. "I'll focus on the Tests, but I'm beyond bored now."

"We're not even one percent done—"

"I won't quit," I think before she suggests it. "So let's just go on."

I do a series of at least a few hundred more Test cycles. Most of the time, Phoe has to intervene in the gruesome scenarios like she did before, but when it comes to logic-leaning Tests, since I learned all the answers, I do them on my own.

After I push the guy off the cliff again and get back to the corridor, I think at Phoe, "I don't want to see that hospital room again. Can you take over my mind from here?"

"I can, but it would be safer to—"

"I think it's worth the risk," I think wearily. "You took over for me so many times already, and nothing happened. I'm just so—"

Phoe must do her takeover thing, because my mind blanks, and I'm standing next to a green door.

"Wow, that was so much easier." I grin. "Can you please, pretty please, do a bunch more? If I experience another—"

"Fine," Phoe thinks before I get the chance to finish, and I black out again.

When I come to, I'm standing next to another green door.

I look to my left and have to rub my eyes in amazement. The row of green doors reaches the horizon, same as the ice ones on my right.

"How many Tests did you take without giving me back control?" I ask Phoe gratefully.

"Too many," she answers sullenly. I expect her to ask if I want to quit, but she doesn't.

"Can you do that again? Pretty please, with sugar on—"

My mind goes dark again.

This time I come to on the cliff. The giant guy is there, so I assume I'm about to hear the train and the screams.

"Figured you'd want to do the honors." Phoe's thought sounds gleeful. "This is the last scenario. Once you push him down, the score will finally reach the number we need. From there, I'll take care of the rest."

I feel a huge wave of gratitude toward Phoe for sparing me the need to do these Tests for the months or years I had left. I didn't want to admit to myself how much I wanted this ordeal over.

On a whim, I raise the watch-Screen to my face, wondering what I'm about to return to, and my insides turn to jelly.

The real-world me is falling. Guard-Theo is frozen in the middle of clutching the disk to his chest as he plummets into the forest.

"It's all under control." Phoe's thought enters my mind defensively. "I warned you about looking at that damn Screen."

"You mean I'll fall to my death after all this?" I can't help but subvocalize. "Is that what you mean by 'under control'?"

"There were Guards chasing your body, so that maneuver couldn't be avoided. As soon as the Test is over, you'll experience me using your muscles to resolve the situation, or if you prefer, I can do what I did here: ride your body without you even being conscious at all. This way you'll regain awareness only after I make sure you don't hit the ground. Hell, I can have you come to *after* all the flying is over."

"Or I might never come to at all," I mumble. "Not if you get me killed."

With effort, I tear my gaze away from the frightening image on the watch-Screen, and at that moment, something catches my attention.

It's the very familiar back of the about-to-be-pushed-off-a-cliff guy. Unlike the thousands of previous times we've gone through this scenario, he's acting differently. The giant is turning toward me.

Shocked, I stare at his front. It looks like it's made out of molten clay—assuming someone used that material to create a monster from a nightmare.

As I blink at him uncomprehendingly, the creature points a giant finger at me and opens his ginormous maw.

I half-expect projectiles to launch at me from the gaping hole of his mouth, but instead, I hear an ear-shattering voice say, "Intruder."

His throat clearly wasn't made for talking, which explains the laconic message.

"Fuck," Phoe says out loud. "It's the anti-intrusion algorithm."

CHAPTER TWENTY-ONE

"It's my fault," I think frantically. "I shouldn't have subvocalized earlier. And I should've been conscious for the Tests instead of—"

"Shut up and focus on this threat," Phoe says, her tone clipped.

The giant steps toward me. His movements shake the ground under my feet.

I take two uncertain steps back, then a few more. When my back is to the edge of the cliff, I hear the train below.

"Shit," I think at Phoe. "When the train hits those five people, I'll fail this scenario, and all this work will be for nothing."

"We'll start with that then," Phoe responds mentally. "Turn around and jump."

Before I even get a chance to express my incredulity at that command, I turn around and jump. For a second, while I'm weightless, I'm uncertain if I jumped because Phoe took over my will or because I now trust her to the point of insanity. Before I fall, a disk materializes under my feet. My shoes transform into the white boots of a Guard, and I connect with the disk. Looks like Phoe wants to make sure I'm magnetically attached to the disk to allow for crazier flight paths.

"I can give you things you encountered in the past," Phoe explains as I whoosh down, heading toward the screaming people. "Like how I gave you the watch."

I do my best not to dwell on the flight down or that the real-world me is actually in a worse situation than I am here, and look back toward the top of the cliff.

Instantly, I wish I hadn't.

The giant is flying behind me. His disk is a copy of mine, but given his size, I wonder if it would be able to carry him in the real world.

Looking forward—or down, if I wanted to be a stickler—I note that the ground is approaching faster than I anticipated. I tense, cold sweat sliding down my back. When we're about six feet from crashing into the railroad tracks, I hear a roar to my right.

I turn toward the sound, thinking my giant pursuer has already landed, but it's worse. The train is literally seconds away from steamrolling over us.

My heartbeat almost drowns out the rumble of the train. In what I assume are my last moments in the Test, I focus on our original targets: the five unfortunate people tied to the rails. I notice details about them that I hadn't before, like how they're tied together by the same thick rope.

"We're jumping off," Phoe informs me when the bottom of my disk is about two feet off the ground.

A bunch of actions happen so fast I have a hard time keeping up, even though I'm the one performing them. I put my fingers together to disable the magnet and jump off the disk. Then I grab the disk by its edge and rush toward the soon-to-be victims. I can't help but notice the handle on the very bottom of the disk, which I didn't see there before. The handle makes the disk look like an ancient shield.

"I improvised a little," Phoe explains.

The train is getting closer.

Stopping next to the tied-up people, I manage to grab a couple of the loose pieces of rope binding them together and tie a tight knot around the shield's handle.

The train is a leap away, and the noise is teeth shattering.

I hover the disk right above the five people, handle down. In a continuous motion, I jump on top of the disk, and as soon as my feet connect with it, I point at the sky.

With five people attached to its bottom, the disk doesn't rocket upward as fast as it usually would, but it does move. Someone below me screams as the chimney of the engine whips by.

Behind me, I hear something that sounds like a mix between a maniacal laugh and a 9.0-magnitude earthquake.

I dare to glance back and see that the giant is about seventy feet away from us.

"I was hoping you would do that and you did." His words sound like tectonic plates colliding. "Now you have no escape."

To highlight his words, he raises his ginormous arms to the sky, and lighting strikes two inches away from my right shoulder.

"He might have a point," Phoe whispers in my ear. "I was hoping that saving these people would register as a pass, but we missed a step: him getting killed. I bet the bastard didn't know that until it happened, but—"

"So we kill him," I think desperately. "That'll get us out."

"You can try," the giant booms, and at the command of his arms, two giant tornados form in the distance. "But you *will* fail."

To punctuate his words, he flamboyantly gestures at the tallest mountain, and its peak explodes in a savage, volcanic eruption, with lava, smoke, and debris spewing all around it. Some of the volcanic rock flies into the nearby tornadoes, changing their color from cloud white to murky black.

"He's too powerful, *and* he can read my thoughts," I scream at Phoe as I zoom away on my disk. "How can he read my thoughts?"

Before Phoe can answer, I look back. The giant figure is shimmering and warping as his disk closes in on us. My passengers scream below me, their heavy bulk slowing my disk.

"Oh no. He's accessing the resources that the Test allocated to emulate you." Phoe's the most worried I've ever heard her. "He just performed a preliminary scan of your memories and is changing his shape in response."

"I will be your worst nightmare," a familiar voice shouts from behind me.

"And *I* will make you wish you were dead," yells a different, yet also familiar voice.

I glance back again, and my stomach sinks. The giant is gone—or more accurately, a creature more savage and terrifying has replaced him. Its arms look like they're made of burned meat, and it possesses two heads. The faces on these heads explain the familiar voices. One is Jeremiah's white-haired visage, while the other wears the canine scowl of my second-least-favorite person in Oasis: Owen. Below the lesions and boils of that horribly twisted double neck, the being shimmers as though its body is made out of small particles that move about.

"Bugs," Jeremiah says with malice that's extreme even for a man who tortured me.

"Centipedes, maggots, locusts, bot flies," Owen adds in his signature hyena voice—a voice now twisted with the same uncanny malevolence. "You name it, I've got it."

"Shit. I knew this thing was buggy, but I didn't expect it to manifest so literally," Phoe says, her mental voice drowning out whatever else the Jeremiah-Owen thing might've said to frighten me. "This is bad, Theo. If I allow him to keep leveraging your resources, he'll know your every move before you make it. He'll use your worst fears against you, as he has already begun to do. We'll lose in minutes, if not seconds." Before I can completely panic, she says, "I want to do something, but I want you to be okay with it. Since part of him is inside your allotted resources, I can fight him there on an algorithmic level, but it would eat up my measly share of those same resources. That means you'll have to fly away *and* figure out how to kill him on your own. My hope is that battling me on that second front will also limit his control over our surrounding environment."

Pushing aside my panic, I study my nemesis as we streak across the sky. Jeremiah's face looks concerned, proving that the creature can and did read my mind and knows what Phoe proposed. He waves his hands at me, and two things happen at once: the distant tornadoes move toward me at increasing speeds, and multi-armed creatures that look like a cross between snakes and spiders swarm the nearest ravine. Thousands upon thousands of the freaky things appear, each holding various weapons in their many appendages.

My breathing goes into hyper speed as I focus straight ahead. "It's not a real choice, Phoe," I manage to say out loud. "Do what you have to do. Just give me something to fight with before you disappear."

Even before I'm done speaking, an object appears in my left hand—a sword that looks like a bolt.

"I guess I didn't have to experience something for real for you to be able to grab it from my memory," I think at Phoe, but she doesn't reply. Her abstract battle with the anti-intrusion thing—Jeremiah-Owen—must've begun.

I peek back at my pursuer to see if there's a discernible change. Owen's face—the face I'm most familiar with—looks like it did long ago, when we were little, after Liam ripped out a huge chunk of the would-be bully's hair. That expression, plus the fact he *isn't* waving his arms to make new forces of nature appear, is a good sign.

Unfortunately, the tornadoes he manifested are getting closer, as is my terribly disgusting two-headed enemy. The people hanging from my disk scream again, and I realize I have to lighten my load to increase my speed.

Swerving, I fly toward the nearest ravine, ignoring the guttural screams of the snake-spider 'people' that Jeremiah-Owen created. To keep my passengers alive, I have to get within a reasonable range of the ravine before I drop them off.

That's my first mistake, because even flying six feet above the snake-spiders' heads is too low for *my* safety. With a whirl of slimy skin, a large snake-spider specimen jumps up, and a few of his smaller friends follow.

In a flash, I take in the abomination. It has eight limbs like a spider, with two hind ones that are longer, serving as makeshift legs, while the front six are more like arms. Its skin looks slimy like a snake's, but its head makes it look like a typical member of the arachnid family. The creature grazes the side of the disk with his mandible, sparking the unpleasant sound of teeth against metal. The smaller half-breeds grab onto my passengers, whose voices are now hoarse from screaming.

"Don't kill those five patsies," Jeremiah's head orders the snake-spider team from a distance. "That will let our guest escape."

He's right. If I get these five people killed, I'll fail this Test, but at least I'll be out of this mess. But what if failing this one scenario is all that's required for the Test to kick me out completely? Then we'll have accomplished nothing. Gritting my teeth, I sit down on the disk. With a careful swing, I use my sword to cut the rope connecting the cargo of scared people to my disk.

With one final ear-piercing cry, the people drop into the almost-caressing tentacles of the snake-spiders. The monsters pass the people along to one another, like the ancients did with stage divers at rock concerts. The five people inevitably make their way to the Jeremiah-Owen creature, which takes them by the rope and flies off. I assume he took them somewhere safe, because he doesn't want the Test to end just yet.

I look down, assessing my next move, and realize the second reason that getting close to the ravine was a potentially fatal mistake.

Bows and arrows are among the many weapons the snake-spider monstrosities are wielding. They have their bows raised in my direction, and sunlight is glinting off a myriad of steel-tipped arrows.

"At least I looked," I think at Phoe out of habit and, suppressing my fear of heights, I point my hand directly at the sky with a pumping motion.

As the disk propels me upward, I hear the whoosh of thousands of arrows. It's as though a giant waterfall is chasing me. My harsh breathing drowns out the sound as I increase my speed with another spasmodic jerk of my hand.

Despite my whiplash-inducing velocity, the arrows are quicker. A hundred or so fly by me on every side, and I hear dozens of them hit the bottom of the disk with a loud metal-on-metal *thump*.

And just when I think I'm in the clear, pain sears through me.

CHAPTER TWENTY-TWO

My eyes tear up, and a twisted scream escapes my throat. With inhuman effort, I resist grabbing my head, knowing that doing so with my left hand will cost me the sword, and doing so with my right will send my disk into a violent tailspin.

In a haze of pain, I understand what must've happened. An arrow clipped my ear. I don't have a mirror to check, but given the severity of the pain, I have to assume the arrow took a chunk of my ear off, if not the whole thing. I fight my body's instinct to go into shock, because that would send me plummeting into the horde of monsters below.

The arrows that missed me fly high into the sky, blotting out the sun and turning the world above me dark, an impression heightened by my agony. As they begin to fall, I understand the new danger: I have to make sure the arrows don't turn me into a porcupine on their way down.

My left hand clutches the sword in the proverbial death grip—which should really be renamed to a 'nearly getting killed' grip. With my right hand, I make a movement that can best be described as attempting to touch my right elbow, something that's more impossible than licking my elbow or touching it with my nose. The impossible gesture translates into a half-summersault that is so violently sudden I would've thrown up if I'd had a morsel of food in my system.

Blood rushes into my head as I fly upside down. The arrows come down, sounding like hail banging against the bottom of the disk. As the arrows continue their downward path, the snake-spiders raise a sea of shields to protect themselves.

The train roars in the distance. I guess the tracks below are still functional.

My blood fights gravity as it tries to leave my face. Putting down their shields, the snake-spiders raise their bows again. I get a good view of every single one of them aiming at me.

The rumble of the train gets louder—too loud given how far we are from the tracks.

The nightmarish archers release their arrows, sending another volley of wooden missiles toward me.

I prepare to reverse my earlier maneuver, when the sound of the train becomes thunderous, and I finally understand.

It's not the train; it's the first of the tornadoes.

In a savage jerk, I'm sucked into the twister, my disk and I instantly spinning like a kamikaze leaf. The arrows get half pulled in, half dispersed by the force of moving air.

I see the world in small slices: a glimpse of snake-spiders flying and screaming inside another twister—the one that's on a collision course with mine; a glimmer of Jeremiah-Owen, watching from the safety of his disk as he flies out of the path of the forces he unleashed; and in my peripheral vision, I see an actual metal train car, as well as ripped-out tracks and rocks twice my size, all randomly swirling around the deadly circle.

The noise is beyond deafening, and the constant rotations make me dry heave.

My knuckles are white from holding on to the bolt-sword through all of this. The only reason I don't let go is my fear that the wind will plunge it right back into me.

My world becomes a game of dodging gigantic, deadly debris. If it weren't for the magnetized shoes, I'd be separated from the disk long ago. As is, I'm glued to it, but it's actually making me thrash around more violently due to its flying capabilities and shape.

I dodge a boulder the size of my head, but a broken arrow whips by and slices my left thigh. I clutch at the bleeding wound, and a burning pain explodes in my right calf muscle. I twist my body and swing the sword, then glance down at my leg. A snake-spider bit into my flesh, but it now has the sword in its eye. I think it's screaming, but it's impossible to hear over the noise of the tornado. As a consequence of it opening its mandibles, my calf is freed, and we instantly fly in different directions.

In the next second, a piece of rail misses my temple by two inches, and I forget all about the pain and my multiplying wounds.

I have to get out of this tornado, or I'll die.

In a desperate attempt to get control over my fate, I even out my hand and the disk by association. Just to make myself fly in a standing position requires all my effort. When I manage it—and by that I mean when my hand goes from shaking violently to only having subdued tremors running through it—I gesture forward.

I bet this is how an ancient surfer would feel like if he ever tried to ride a tsunami. Eventually, though, I get the knack for riding the wind and fly up and away from the eye of the tornado. Only when I reach the very edge of the wind tunnel do I realize my miscalculation. As I rotated inside the whirlpool of air, its centrifugal forces—or whatever the right term is—increased my speed. This becomes especially clear when I exit the horrid wind tunnel and get propelled toward the ravine at the speed of an overzealous bullet.

Arrows fly at me. Not in a cloud like before, but a few stray ones. Down below, I see that I'm approaching the ravine. I clench my fingers into a tight fist—a stopping gesture Phoe taught me. Sparks fly as the edge of the disk connects with the rock.

If Phoe weren't busy, I'd suspect she was doing the next move for me. I touch all my right fingers together at the same time as I let go of the sword. The result is that the magnetic pull of the disk goes away and the inertia of the impact makes me slide down and fall on my side. I tumble and scrape the skin on my hands and arms as I try to stop the momentum from carrying me forward. It occurs to me that if I hadn't gotten separated from the disk, the jerk of the crash could have broken my legs. If I'd held on to the sword, I probably would've skewered myself like a human shish kebab during this already-unpleasant roll.

I finally come to a stop. Blood pounds in my temples, and my body feels like it's gone through an ancient meat grinder. I'm tempted to lie here and let something kill me, but I can't let that happen.

I struggle onto my feet and look around.

The disk is at least a dozen feet away, meaning my tumble away from it was longer than I realized.

Unfortunately, twenty or thirty feet away is a small group of snake-spider creatures, and they're running toward me. The tornado did a number on them too. They don't have all their usual weapons, they're missing their shields, and they look flustered. Then again, I have no idea what these things look like when they're nice and calm.

Jeremiah-Owen is flying my way. He's near the smoke of the volcano he unleashed.

I will the volcano to explode again, but it ignores me.

At least the tornadoes are traveling away from us, though it would be better if one of them took Jeremiah-Owen with it.

I launch into my best approximation of a sprint, suppressing a cry every time I step with my injured right leg. To make matters worse, blood is oozing from the bite in my calf and the million cuts all over my body, and the pulse of agony from what used to be my ear is only increasing.

The fastest snake person is two feet away from me when I reach for the disk, grabbing it by the handle that Phoe created to tie the rope to.

The snake people stop and pull back their arrows.

I again raise the disk like a medieval shield.

Two arrows hit it and fall harmlessly to the ground. The rest of the arrows overshoot me.

I don't get a chance to celebrate not getting skewered, because the first attacker is already here, its breath smelling worse than that pile of fecal matter from Owen's prank. Without much thought, I hit the snake-spider's head with the disk. The metal-on-mandible impact sends pain ricocheting down my right arm. My attacker staggers back, giving me a window to grab my bolt-sword off the ground.

Seeing my weapon, the wounded monster readies its curved blade.

I catch its strike on my makeshift shield and bring the bolt-sword down on its wrist.

The good news is that the snake-spider is now missing an arm. The bad news is it has five more left. The worse news is that one of those arms is attempting to catch the falling sword.

In a flurry of motion, I smack my shield into that arm. I can't let it get the weapon. Then, capitalizing on the creature's momentary daze, I cleave off its head. A fountain of pale blue blood gushes out of its neck. I guess in that way, the creatures are more spider-like than snake-like, since a snake's blood would be red.

Its body hits the ground, revealing two more of its cousins about to catch up with me. Behind those two, I see something that makes me pause.

A cloud of bugs—my guess is locusts—streams from Jeremiah-Owen's bug-infested body. The man—and I use that term loosely—is flying parallel to the bottom of the ravine. Where his bugs pass, any remaining snake-spider people scream like rabid banshees. Great. The bugs must not be real locusts; according to what I've read, those were herbivores, and these grasshopper-looking things are obviously flesh eaters.

"See, Why-Odor, we're keeping you alive," says the anti-intrusion creature's Owen-head in a voice so loud it even silences the dying screams of the locusts' victims.

"So we can do what we decided," Jeremiah's head pipes in just as loudly. "*Then* he can come out and die."

"Of course," Owen agrees. "And what a genius idea we had, if we do say so—"

I ignore the rest of their nonsensical conversation, because the two eight-limbed attackers are right in front of me. The larger one swats a curved blade at my side.

I bring my shield-disk up to absorb the blow.

The smaller attacker thrusts its sword at me. I parry with mine.

I know I have to do something to turn the situation in my favor. I can barely fight one of these things, so two of them will kill me twice as fast.

The larger snake-spider swats its sword at my legs, while the smaller one strikes at my left shoulder.

I jump. The larger enemy's sword slices a thin gash into my white Guard boot. Simultaneously, I smash the disk into the larger creature's face and clink my sword against the smaller attacker's blade.

The larger enemy is stunned, but the smaller one manages to grab my left wrist in one of its spare limbs.

Though I've thought of it as the smaller one, I meant it purely in reference to its currently stunned cousin. Compared to me, the thing is huge. Its grip on my wrist is like a vise.

With all my remaining strength, I bring the shield down on its limb. As soon as its grip loosens, I twist my wrist, cleaving off one of the arms in a splash of blue blood.

I see movement out of the corner of my eye and instinctively meet it with the shield. It turns out to be the larger opponent. It clearly recovered. Hoping the block stunned it, I strike out with my sword. It catches the blade with two of its hands. The blade leaves streaks of blue blood on the creature's palms, but it doesn't let go. The smaller creature seizes the moment, drops on its remaining legs, and kicks me with its leg-like hind limbs. It hits me in the chest, and the impact is so powerful I fly backward, landing painfully on my back. The agony is overwhelming, forcing me to drop both the sword and the disk.

The creatures approach me, menace gleaming in the slit pupils of their green snake eyes.

I roll over to where I dropped the disk and jump on it, scrambling to my feet. The adrenaline rush makes me forget about my injuries.

The smaller snake-spider takes its bow from its shoulder and reaches for an arrow.

The larger one throws its sword at me.

I attempt to duck under the projectile but feel a blast of burning heat in the side of my head. The sword clanks far behind me, so I assume it just grazed my head, though it feels like I got scalped.

Through the pain and as though in slow motion, I watch the smaller snake-spider pull the bowstring, aiming at my midsection.

It doesn't get a chance to let go of its bowstring.

The smaller snake-spider screams, and its larger comrade joins in.

The locusts only take a few seconds, but they leave nothing of my attackers behind as they continue their flight. I use those two seconds to recover my sword from the ground, but I don't get a chance to activate my disk.

A swarm—though the proper term may be a plague—of locust-like insects flies toward me.

Their buzzing reverberates in the metal of the disk under my feet. They form a circle around me, blocking the sky.

Then a large locust—perhaps the leader—zooms toward me and takes a bite out of my cheek.

Nauseated by terror, I swat at him with my sword.

The rest of the bugs screech-buzz excitedly.

My sword misses the tiny attacker, and his friends take that as a sign that I'm edible and harmless.

As one, they swarm toward me.

CHAPTER TWENTY-THREE

"Stop, little ones," Jeremiah's head booms.

The locusts stop an inch away from my skin. Their mandibles click in a collective cacophony of hungry frustration.

"Yeah," Owen's head agrees. "As fun as it would be to see you eat this intruder alive, allowing him to die means his real-world self won't remember any of this."

"Right, which is why we have something more permanent in mind," Jeremiah's head says.

"Minds," corrects Owen's head. "As in plural."

"We're part of the same entity, so singular," responds Jeremiah's head, but he doesn't sound certain.

"But you said *we* have something in mind," Owen's head objects.

"Irrelevant," Jeremiah's head says impatiently. "Make way for your friends," he says sternly—to the locusts, I assume.

The locusts form a small opening in their plague.

A new kind of buzzing ensues in the distance, and within moments, the inner circle of locusts is filled with flies.

"Do your job," Owen's head says in his excited hyena voice.

I assume he was talking to the flies, because they attack me.

When they land on me, I don't feel any pain. Maybe the existing sting and burn of my wounds is masking the damage they're inflicting. However, panic and disgust kick in when I feel a dozen flies crawling into my throbbing ear.

I extend my hand, palm up, and activate my disk. As soon as I'm floating, I judder my hand in random directions. As I fly through the locusts, I swing my sword around to clear the way.

The locusts can't keep me trapped without eating me, so I push through their wall and come out on the other side in an explosion of angry buzzing. The locusts don't pursue me en mass.

Frantically, I fly toward the volcano. In an ancient book, I read something about insects, specifically bees, not being fond of smoke. Since the fiery mountain is still spewing smoke, it seems like a good destination.

Even before I enter the smoke zone, the number of flies on my body greatly decreases. They're having trouble flying as fast as me.

Maddened by the few flies still crawling in my head, I increase my speed. If the smoke doesn't get rid of them, I'll have to stick the sword in my ear.

When the smoke envelops me, the flies in my ear finally exit, buzzing loudly as they go.

The flies are pretty much gone, and the locusts don't want to pursue me into this smoggy area either. I breathe in a sigh of relief, but the feeling is short-lived. The insects didn't follow me here for a good reason. I do my best to cough out the copious amounts of smoke I inhaled, my eyes watering as I fight a wave of dizziness.

"It's done," Jeremiah says from somewhere nearby.

Through the smoke, I spot my two-headed nemesis and get an unwelcome look at his bug-infested body. He followed me here. Looking at the disgusting mess of insects, I find a rare reason to be grateful to live in Oasis: those critters are absent from our little habitat.

Fortunately, the smoke is forcing the creepy crawlies to hide in the folds of Jeremiah-Owen's torso. Unfortunately, that same smoke is threatening my survival. Even worse, my enemy is holding a curved sword that must've belonged to one of the snake-spiders.

"He doesn't understand. He probably thinks he's out of trouble," Owen's head complains annoyingly. "We should tell him."

"True," Jeremiah's head responds. Then, turning to me, he says, "Those flies you came into contact with are our interpretation of the bot variety. If it isn't clear, they laid their eggs all over your body."

My hands and feet go ice cold, and bile rises in my throat.

"That's right," Owen's head echoes. "Unlike your regular dermatobia hominis, the larvae of these beauties take seconds to form and wake with a voracious appetite."

My overwhelming revulsion and horror temporarily suppress my ability to speak.

"I think he's beginning to get it," Owen's head says. "But not fully, I think."

My body itches all over, though the reaction could be psychosomatic.

"I'll be happy to explain," Jeremiah's head says. "Don't worry about them spreading throughout your body. There's a specific task we're having them take care of. We instructed them to eat specific regions of your brain. The damage will stay with you when you exit the Test. That is how the synchronization between your current state and your physical neurons works."

Though I heard his words, they're so terrifying I don't want to accept their meaning.

Owen's head adds excitedly, "Right now, they're munching on the parts of your brain responsible for face recognition, starting with the so-called fusiform face area. And before you ask, you won't feel them doing this. Unfortunately, the human brain doesn't have pain receptors, but rest assured, they are—"

I don't wait for him to finish. Despite his assurances, I *do* feel something crawling inside my head. With a violent, animalistic roar, I point my hand at the two-headed creature and torpedo the disk forward.

My plan is simple: I need to kill Jeremiah-Owen before my brain is irreparably damaged. If I kill him, the Test will register that as a score.

"He wants to have fun as we wait for the damage to set in," Owen's head says with a giggle, and the two-headed monster flies toward me on his disk. The trail of smoke and bugs behind the creature makes him look like a nightmarish comet.

As we get closer, I focus on the path of his sword.

When we're almost at the striking range, I expect him to stop, but he doesn't, so I don't bother braking either. It looks like this will be a surreal flying version of a jousting match.

In the fraction of a second it takes us to pass each other, I look for an opening.

Only the two necks, the hands, and the feet of the creature look human enough to injure. The right arm is controlling his flight, so I strike it. My blade touches something soft, followed by a clanking of metal on metal as we zoom past each other.

"That hurt," Owen's head whines as I turn around.

A streak of blood stains Jeremiah-Owen's wrist, but the wound isn't bad enough to impede him from controlling his disk. My opponent cautiously circles around and gesticulates at me, droplets of blood spraying in every direction. I swerve and propel my disk forward, my sword ready. Our swords meet with a painful ricochet, but neither of us injures the other.

Despite not hurting Jeremiah-Owen, I did glean something important: my enemy can't turn his disk at as steep of an angle as I can. It's probably because he's standing barefoot, without the magnetic assistance I have. I tilt my hand sideways, which translates to me flying with my body parallel to the ground.

I whoosh past my opponent and strike his left shoulder, killing a number of bugs without damaging their host in any noticeable way. The key thing is that I come out unscathed, proving that flying sideways is indeed a promising strategy.

An extreme bout of nausea and lightheadedness hits me. Did I inhale too much smoke? Am I about to pass out? Should I make my way outside the volcano's reach?

I look at my opponent, and my stomach fills with solid mercury.

The two heads are unfamiliar.

No, that's not true. It's their *faces* that are unfamiliar.

"It's happening, isn't it?" says the gray-haired head with Jeremiah's voice. "You can't recognize me, can you?"

I look from one unfamiliar face to the other. The feeling I have is different from looking at faces of people whose names I don't know. It's as though the faces are illusory and blurry. The facial features don't add up to make a face, rendering their countenance unrecognizable as faces. I know the round circle with leathery skin and white hair is Jeremiah's head and the other one is Owen's, but that's not what I experience when I look at them.

Did Phoe's control over the anti-intrusion algorithm fail? Did it simply change its faces to worry me? It doesn't seem likely, because if the thing could shape-shift, it would first change our environment to unleash new elemental forces against me. Which leaves only the explanation he gave me.

Part of my mind is now damaged, and I won't be able to recognize faces anymore, even outside the Test.

This concept is as strange as it is horrifying. I imagine what it would be like to walk down the Institute and not recognize any of the Youths. I'll seem rude to my acquaintances. When they speak to me, I won't know who I'm talking to. With a sinking feeling, I think about not recognizing Liam and Phoe. The idea that I'll no longer enjoy looking at Phoe's face is—

"Now that you know what our larvae can do, let me tell you how you're going to die," Jeremiah says gleefully. "You see, in your mind, we saw your condition on the outside world. You're falling, and you'll need to act swiftly with your hands to save yourself."

"Let me tell him the best part." Owen's voice is brimming with excitement. "Our hungry little friends are now eating the parts of your brain that control your arms—"

"—so you'll die within seconds after we send you back," Jeremiah continues. "You'll try to use your hands to prevent yourself from falling, and you'll fail."

"Even your friend can't move your arms if your motor cortex is damaged. She can only work with what's there," Owen finishes.

Trying to suppress my terror, I look at my Screen-watch. My outside self is still falling. If Jeremiah-Owen is telling the truth, I won't survive the fall.

The Screen goes blank, and Phoe's words appear: *Your only chance is to kill him before the larvae do what he said. I'm sorry I can't help. If I let go on my end, the anti-intrusion algorithm will become impossibly powerful again, making an already-bad situation worse.*

I look away from the watch, my jaw muscles like coiled springs.

Knowing I'm on the brink of real death awakens something ugly and primal in me. I scream and direct my disk to fly at the epicenter of my growing hatred: the two-headed *thing* I'd like to rip to shreds.

Like a flying virtuoso, I swerve left and right as the distance between me and Jeremiah-Owen shrinks. I stay sideways to make it hard for my opponent to strike me. In a blur, he rotates his right arm, ready to thrust it forward. His sword hand goes for my ankle. I let his sword connect with my flesh and channel the resulting blast of pain and adrenaline into my strike. My sword cuts into his right wrist, screeching against bone, and comes out on the other side.

Both heads yelp in pain, and as I fly away, I watch the severed hand plunge into the volcano's depths.

My opponent has two choices: he can let go of his weapon and flee—assuming he can use his left hand to control the disk—or he can stand his ground and fight me as I circle him. I don't let him choose the cowardly option. Gritting my teeth against the overwhelming pain in my calf, I fly up, then down, swooping in on Jeremiah-Owen with my sword raised.

I feel bloodthirsty excitement as my sword cuts deep into my foe's neck. Both mouths scream, but the younger one quiets in a gurgle of agony. With grim satisfaction, I realize I've severed it. With a clank against the metal disk, Owen's head rolls over and falls down into the depth of the volcano below. A fountain of red blood gushes from the stump of his neck.

My elation at the sight of blood and Jeremiah's screams frighten the sheltered Oasis part of me, but the wild ancient inside me revels in the knowledge that I'm about to kill my enemy. All I need to do is cut off one more head.

A bout of nausea hits me again.

I try to turn my right wrist sideways.

My arm doesn't respond. The larvae must've already damaged the part of my brain responsible for its control.

Frantically, I test my control over my left hand. This hand is still mine to wield.

Time slows down. Faster than the speed of thought, I form a truly desperate plan. Not giving my rational side a chance to raise any objections, I let go of the sword in my left hand to navigate the disk.

Nothing happens. The disk control must be a right-hand thing, which makes sense. How else would the disk know which hand to obey? Adjusting my plan, I grab my right arm with my still-functioning left and point it at the one-headed monster.

Jerking my right hand with the aid of my left, I propel forward.

Jeremiah's head stops screaming.

He clumsily readies his sword.

I increase my speed.

Though I don't recognize Jeremiah's face as a combined entity, I do recognize individual features. His eyes, wide with dilated pupils, stand out.

I raise my arms high and slam into him, ignoring his sword. The sword enters my side, bringing with it an unbearable coldness.

There's no pain, but I know it's coming, so I hurry. I grab my enemy in a bear hug, pushing the sword deeper into my side. My hands meet behind his back, and I use my left hand to collect all the fingers of my right into the disable-magnet gesture.

When my fingers come together, the pain from the sword impaling my side spreads through my body with the intensity of the tornado I escaped.

Before the pain undoes my will, I clasp my hands in an unbreakable grip and jump off my disk with one last powerful push of my feet.

I fall like a rock, bringing my enemy down with me. Our disks hover serenely above us as we plummet.

The pain starts in earnest, and I scream, my vision blurring.

Jeremiah's head is screaming louder than I am. His bugs separate from his torso and sting me wherever they can.

I think I respond with a maniacal laugh, though I might be hysterically screaming. They can sting me all they want. My macabre work is done. We're falling into the boiling lava.

I'm not sure if the heat I feel is from the lava or the poison of the multiple insect bites. I'm on the brink of losing consciousness from all this torment, but oblivion doesn't come.

It's amazing how many thoughts go through my mind during the fall that lasts only a heartbeat. I will accomplish my goal of killing the Jeremiah-Owen creature and earn that last point on my Test score. I also understand the cost: I'm about to die. This me.

The in-Test me. The me who's been changed by taking this Test. The me who's capable of this kind of sacrifice—an act my outside self might not even comprehend without all these memories. The me who's so afraid to be forgotten, to cease to exist—

The monster screaming with Jeremiah's voice bursts into flames in my arms. The world becomes fire. The burning is unbearable. I try to scream again, but we get so close to the lava that the world goes out in a flash of fire.

CHAPTER TWENTY-FOUR

I'm falling.

Instead of waking up in the bed in the black building, I'm in the sky over the pine forest.

I'm clutching a flying disk to my chest. My wrists twist in a throwing maneuver that's all too familiar. I did this move the last time Phoe chose to have me fall with the disk clutched to my chest.

Like last time, the disk is instantly under my feet, and I fly away from the dozen Guards pursuing me. Thanks to the fall, I have a big lead on them—the point of the insanity I just lived through.

Now that I'm not weightless, questions spring to mind: Why am I actually here? Where is *here?* Am I inside the Test? The last thing I recall is lying down to sleep to initiate the Test.

Something materializes in front of me. It's a being of light and power, like an angel or deity. I've seen this too-beautiful-for-mortal-eyes sight once before, in my cave after I got Phoe the resources of the IRES game. She looks the same way now, only we're here in the real world—if that's where we are.

"Oops," she booms in that too-sacred-for-mortal-ears voice. "This is an accident." In her normal voice, she adds, "I just got the resources from the Test. It's magnificent, Theo. I don't know how I can ever repay you."

She once again looks like her pixie-haired self, and the meaning of her words penetrates my adrenaline-clouded brain.

"The Test is over?" I suck in a breath to calm my racing heartbeat. "How? Are you sure this isn't it, right now? Is this like that IRES game's trick where it wanted me to think it was reality?"

"The Test doesn't work like that, and I told you so before you started it," Phoe says urgently. "Go to your cave. I'll deal with the Guards without your consciousness. I'll explain everything there."

I show my pursuers two middle fingers, and a white tunnel takes me to our favorite VR hangout. I appear between a dinosaur skeleton and a giant one-eyed teddy bear.

Phoe waves, and the area clears. A plush chair appears, and I gladly sit on it. Phoe chooses to sit on her own chair across from me.

Between us, on the holographic display Phoe likes to use to show the outside world, I watch Guard-Theo fly away from his dozen pursuers.

"The Test happened, Theo," Phoe begins. "And now that it's over, I'm well positioned to take advantage of the coming opportunity to fix things. As we wait for it, let me tell you what happened."

She proceeds to tell me about the Test: the ethical and logical dilemmas, the battle with the anti-virus-like protector, and the horrific way I lost all memory of the whole ordeal.

"I can't believe I could've lost the ability to recognize faces and my control over my arms," I whisper. "Was that creature telling the truth?"

"Yes. You likely would've died had you not killed yourself in the Test. If your Test self had been written back onto your current consciousness, the damage to your motor regions would've prevented both you and me from dealing with the fall in that critical moment. Of course, had you survived, the damage you suffered in the Test might not have been permanent. For one, you might've gotten some functionality back due to natural neuroplasticity, which allows new brain regions to take care of ones that get damaged. Also, I could've used your nanocytes to compensate for lost—"

"That's enough." I put my hand on hers and keep it there. There's an ache in my chest. I came so close to dying, and a part of me did die—the in-Test Theo that I don't remember.

Phoe looks at me, her eyes filled with sadness. "I warned you, back there in the Test, but you didn't listen."

"I'm sure I had good reasons," I say uncertainly. "Though it's hard to believe I could do something so—"

"You did it for me, and I should never have allowed it." Phoe turns her hand to grab mine and squeezes my palm. "I'm so sorry."

Now I feel bad for upsetting her. "Look, Phoe, I'm fine," I say. "You got the resources you needed. It's just a few memories. Besides, if you're so worried about it, can't you plant those memories in my head the way you did with that Pi Trojan thing?"

"No, that wouldn't be the same since I can't give you the exact memories you lost," she says.

"And I don't really want to remember the kind of pain my Test alter ego must've gone through," I mumble.

We sit in silence for a few minutes, just looking at each other. Finally, I say, "Listen, what's done is done. The key thing is that you got the resources, right?"

"Yes. Once your score was sent out, the Test system tried to permanently store that super-large value in a variable that was much too small. The buffer overloaded, as I hoped it would, and that allowed me to inject my own code and bring the whole system down. I'll bring it back up for a day next year, so the Elderly-to-be can take the Test on the next Birth Day without anyone being the wiser." Excitement dances in her eyes as she says, "You have no idea what I'm capable of now. The Test was a resources glut. More than I ever suspected. My new capabilities are—"

"So why are the Guards still chasing me?" I wave at the hologram. "Can't you use your super resources to control those guys without the Envoy learning about it? For that matter, have you learned what the Envoy is?"

Phoe scratches her blond spikes and says, "I'm waiting for an opportune moment to deal with the Guards. A Forgetting is about to begin, and when it does, I'll highjack it to make the right people Forget anything having to do with our misadventures today. Since it will seem to be part of a sanctioned Forgetting, the Envoy will not learn of it."

"But who was Forgotten—" I begin to ask, but she shushes me and gestures at the hologram, which grows brighter in response.

Guard-Theo is descending quickly, while the crew of Guards chasing him suddenly stops mid-air.

"The Forgetting is happening. They don't remember what they're doing there anymore," Phoe says smugly. "I need you to take care of one last loose end before I give you all the answers. Even with my prodigious resources, I can't control your body in that building."

On the hologram, my real-world self just landed next to the Quietude building.

"Do the gesture to get back," Phoe commands. "Our Forgetting window is small."

I do as she says, and after a whirlwind of white, I find myself standing there, next to the gray doors of the Witch Prison.

"Now go. Get the trapped Guard out of there and give him back his uniform," Phoe whispers. "The answers are coming."

"Fine," I think and walk into the corridor.

It takes minutes to get to the room in question.

Phoe's ghostly Screen is nowhere in sight, but the door opens at my command. She must've already undone the jam she created earlier.

"Finally," the Guard says. "There's been a terrible—"

When he sees me ready my Stun Stick, his eyes widen and he falls silent for a second. Then he says through his teeth, "*You*. You won't get away with—"

"Shut up, Noah," I say and zap him.

Since no Screen from Phoe shows up to tell me which way to go, I drag my victim the same way I came from. I don't come across anyone on the way, which I guess is normal given the time of day. If I had, I'd probably be dragging more bodies.

"Swap clothes with him," Phoe says when I come out. "Hurry up. The less surveillance footage I have to delete, the better."

My helmet snaps off, as do other parts of my suit.

I take everything off. Phoe watches with fascination.

"You just wanted to see me naked," I mumble as I swiftly pull up my Birth-Day-edition blue pants.

She grins and says, "I've seen your stuff before. Now back to your cave, and maybe I'll show you mine as a way to make amends."

I flush—and not from the obscene gesture I'm forced to execute.

After yet another psychedelic white display, I'm standing between a shark tank and a pile of dynamite someplace deep inside my man cave.

We return to our cushy chairs and sit down.

On that same holographic display, I watch my real-world self walking somewhere, obviously under Phoe's control.

"We're walking to your room," she answers my question before I get a chance to ask it. "I want you in bed early today."

"What about—"

"Noah already Forgot that you ever attacked him."

"And—"

"You're not in trouble anymore," Phoe says.

"How about—"

"It's complicated," she says. "Like I started saying, the only thing I can't do is penetrate that cursed Firewall. Still, I think I have a pretty good guess as to what the Envoy is, but I don't want to share this until I get proof, which I'll have within minutes. For now, you still have some catching up to do, as you don't know what happened in the real world during the Test. Due to the time differences, it's only been a short while, but it was *very* eventful."

"Oh, right, we were being—"

"—chased by the Guards for a good reason." Phoe crosses her legs, catches me staring, and gives me a mischievous wink.

"How—"

"The subjective time in the Test was many, many years, though your poor in-Test self wasn't cognizant of that time once I started taking the Tests for him. Here, it's been less than an hour."

"Wait," I say. "How did you know I was going to ask about that? Are you finishing my thoughts before I even express them? I noticed—"

"Yes, that's what I'm doing." Phoe's speaking so fast I have trouble keeping up. "Predicting most of your thoughts is trivial for me, given my new resources. I have the bandwidth to—"

"Can you please *not* do it? It's eerie." I rub my temples, wondering if she knows what I'm about to say next. "It makes me feel like I don't have a choice about what I'll say or think."

"Sure," Phoe says, at a more normal speed this time. "I merely thought to speed up our communication, given how much you're dying to get those answers. Besides, the very fact you asked me to stop doing something proves I didn't anticipate your reaction, else I wouldn't have started finishing your sentences. Anyway, I can also tell you don't want to discuss free will."

I scratch the bridge of my nose, narrow my eyes, and say, "Let me finish my thoughts."

"Agreed," she says.

"Now please answer one of my questions."

"Okay." She gets up and paces. "I'm trying to decide where to start."

"How about at the beginning?" I can't help but say sarcastically. "Tell me what happened to get those Guards to chase us."

"It's not so simple," she says. "But fine, here goes. I won't just tell you. I'll show you."

A large Screen appears in front of me.

Jeremiah is standing next to an antique wood table in an unusual room filled with ancient relics. The old man is no longer wearing his helmet, but he still has the rest of the Guard suit on.

On the table in front of him are two long-stemmed glasses made of crystal. They look like wine cups from ancient movies. Jeremiah takes a small box from the table and empties its contents into the glass to his right. Whatever he puts inside the glass is nearly invisible.

Phoe freezes the recording with a gesture and says, “I’m not sure what to show you next. He’s about to change into normal clothes, and I have two options as to how to continue.”

“What’s that stuff he put in the glass?” I lean closer to the Screen, hoping to read any writing on the box.

“It’s called cyanide—one of those friendly ancient discoveries. It’s a powerful poison. Whoever drinks from that cup will die.”

“Who—”

“Just watch,” she says and gestures.

The Screen comes to life again.

Jeremiah is dressed in an intricate costume. He’s holding an ancient-looking bottle.

Someone knocks on the door.

“Come in, please,” Jeremiah says, his voice unusually friendly.

The door opens, and Fiona walks in.

CHAPTER TWENTY-FIVE

Fiona is dressed as nicely as Jeremiah, her neck adorned with a golden necklace and her white hair braided intricately. She looks at Jeremiah, then looks at the bottle in his hands, then at the glasses, and her cold eyes show a glimmer of warmth.

"Jeremiah?" she says. "What's this about?"

He gestures toward the cup, smiles at her sadly, and says, "That my offer of goodwill surprises you proves my instincts were right. There's too much tension between us—the two most influential people on the Council."

At his ingratiating words, Fiona straightens and walks toward the table.

Capitalizing on his success, Jeremiah pulls the cork out of the wine bottle and pours two glasses. "This here isn't something the Culinary Anthropologists made up." He picks up the leftmost glass and inhales the scent of the drink. "This is the real deal—authentic, ancient wine."

Fiona walks up to the table and takes the rightmost glass by the thin stem and says, "If you think this bribe will change my mind regarding Theodore . . ."

I tense in my chair.

"This is just a peace offering, nothing more. We deserve a bit of Birth Day celebration, after all." He makes the ancient ceremonial gesture for a toast. "I agree to let the Council decide Theodore's fate."

Fiona relaxes and lifts her glass to her mouth.

The picture pauses, and Phoe says, "Oh, I forgot to tell you. By this point, Jeremiah has seen the video where Fiona wants to quit the Council. She has not yet seen the video of Jeremiah cursing and smacking her, or else she might've been more careful."

"Wait, Phoe—" I start to say, but my friend continues the recording, and I stop talking, unable to peel my eyes from the Screen.

Jeremiah sips his wine and grunts approvingly. "Hard to see why alcohol ruined so many lives in antiquity," he says.

Fiona takes a tiny sip of her wine and says, "It's exquisite. Thank—"

She doesn't finish her sentence because Jeremiah does a cleanup gesture at her glass, his own glass, and then the bottle. All three objects disappear.

"What are you doing?" Fiona frowns. "What's the meaning of this?"

"I'm getting rid of the evidence. When I make myself Forget this, I want no clues as to what transpired," Jeremiah replies, his tone even.

"I don't understand. Why would you want to make yourself Forget this nice gesture?" she asks, her eyes widening.

"Quickly," Jeremiah says. "Tell me, when did you last sleep? Did you nap today?"

"No." Fiona gives him a baffled look. "The last time I slept was last night. What does that have to do with anything? Is this some kind of Birth Day joke?"

Jeremiah appears relieved at her words. "I just wanted to know how much of today's events you'll remember after you ascend to Haven."

"Haven?" Fiona's already-pale face turns pure white.

"Yes, that's where you're headed," Jeremiah says, his voice subdued. "I just poisoned you."

"You did what?" she hisses and closes the distance between them.

I squeeze the armrests of my chair so tightly that my hands cramp up. It looks like Phoe's fake video is about to become reality—only in this case, it'll be Fiona smacking Jeremiah.

To Fiona's and my surprise, Jeremiah steps toward her. Before she understands what's going on, he grabs her shoulders and holds her at bay with his much-longer arms. He looks into her eyes, his own gaze the epitome of sadness.

In a soft voice, he says, "Look. We've been at each other's throats since we joined the Council. I always thought you principled, if stubborn, and deserving of respect. This latest act of yours, however, is unforgivable. Making the Council Forget a meeting, making *me,* the Keeper, Forget over some stupid outburst goes against everything the Council stands for. It goes against everything *you* once stood for. I know you probably made yourself Forget, as I will make myself Forget killing you, but I can't let you go on any longer. Sometimes the Keeper must bypass the Council and take matters into his own—"

Before he can utter the last word, Jeremiah pales. Letting go of Fiona, he clutches his throat. His eyes roll into his head, and he collapses. His body disintegrates, molecule by molecule, the way Mason's did when Jeremiah killed him.

I watch in stunned incomprehension. "What the hell was that?" I finally manage to ask.

"His body's resources are automatically reclaimed by the nano—"

"No, I mean, why did he fall instead of Fiona? And how could you let him try to kill her? You said you'd look out for—"

"Hold on," Phoe says. "Let me rewind."

The Screen flickers the scene backward too quickly for me to follow. The video is back to the moment when Jeremiah stepped out of the room, leaving the two wine glasses on the table.

Nothing happens for a few moments. When I'm about to ask Phoe what I'm looking at, the door to the room opens, and a Guard walks in. He walks up to the table and swaps the rightmost cup for the leftmost.

That explains things. Unknowingly, Jeremiah drank his own poison. And that Guard must be—

"Yes, it's you," Phoe says. "Or me, or whatever the right term is. While you were taking the Test, I kept an eye on our friends here. I *did* promise to take care of her, after all. Since I had control of your body, I walked it from the black building to that room"—she points at the Screen—"as soon as I realized what he was about to do. This is, by the way, how I picked up the Guard tail we shook off."

"So the Forgetting you hijacked—it was Jeremiah's?" I relax a little.

"Correct. I weaved my own instructions into Jeremiah's Forgetting—which Fiona initiated soon after he died as a matter of protocol. All but one person, besides you, remembers what transpired today." Phoe waves at the Screen again.

"Who's this other person?" I ask but realize she's already answering my question by playing something on the Screen.

Phoe winks at me and turns toward the Screen.

Fiona is on the Screen. She stands there in her usual spot, surrounded by the Council.

"As the new Keeper, my first order of business is to reassure you all that the investigation the prior Keeper and I initiated is complete."

Hushed murmurs move among the crowd.

A thin, unhealthy-looking Councilor stands and asks, "Is this message coming from the Envoy?"

Fiona's eyes glint with ice as she says, "I will meet with the Envoy shortly. I'm sure he will agree with my decision."

Phoe pauses the video and says, "When she tried to figure out why Jeremiah would attempt to kill her, she came across my fake video—the one implicating Jeremiah. This is why she considers the investigation over. She figures Jeremiah was the culprit."

Before I get a chance to question her, Phoe resumes the video.

"It's my duty as the Keeper to warn you: I will make you Forget about the investigation so you can—"

Phoe stops the video. "That takes care of pretty much all the loose ends except for Fiona."

"Right, but that's one big loose end. Fiona knows about my neural scan being out of whack. Can't you make *her* Forget so everything is really over?"

"Doing so would be too risky. She's the new Keeper and messing with her mind might raise red flags."

"But—"

"Don't worry. I suspect I won't need to do anything anyway. She's talking to the Envoy—"

"Wait. About that. Nothing is over until we know who or what the Envoy is," I say urgently. "He still knows about the investigation. I think it's time you explain—"

"I don't need to explain," Phoe says. "I can show it to you, since, as I was trying to tell you, their conversation is happening as we speak."

I stand up. "What conversation? Are you torturing me on purpose?"

"You didn't want me to answer questions before you asked them. Now you want me to predict what you want to know and tell it to you?" Phoe pouts. "Fine. You heard Fiona. She told them she and the Envoy were meeting. That meeting started a few minutes ago. I can show it to you. So far, it confirms all of my suspicions—suspicions I developed once I smartened up, thanks to the resources of the Test."

"Yes, please show me." My mouth is dry as I add, "Now."

In reply, Phoe makes the orchestra-conductor gesture. My vision and hearing blur into white noise. It's the same thing that happened when she took me to the cathedral-like place where Jeremiah met with the Envoy what feels like years ago.

My senses clear, and I see that I was right. I'm surrounded by the magnificent space, with music blasting like last time. Only instead of organ music, it sounds stringy.

"It's Bach again. His *Cello Suite No. 1, The Prelude*," Phoe whispers. "I'm showing you a recording that's only a few minutes old. They're still talking, you see."

"Who?"

Phoe shows up next to me and points to a slender, white-hooded figure kneeling next to the big stage, where the Envoy last appeared.

It's Fiona, which of course makes sense. She's the new Keeper, and the Keeper gets to meet with the Envoy.

Bright rays of light spread out from the middle of the platform. I cover my face and wait. This happened last time too. The Envoy likes to make an entrance.

When the light subsides, I look at the stage.

A luminous figure is standing there, but it's not the Envoy. More accurately, it's not the same Envoy. The being clearly shares similarities with the guy I called the Envoy before, and they're of the same species, as it were, but this is a different specimen. The wings of this being don't have feathers and look more like the wings of an albino bat. This figure also lacks some of the confident majesty of the other one, and he's wearing some kind of short britches or capri pants rather than a loincloth. As with the previous one, his torso leaves no doubt that this Envoy is male, though he isn't as well built.

Fiona pulls the cowl from her head and studies the face of the visitor. Something about his face both fascinates and upsets her.

This Envoy's replacement has a young face like that of his predecessor's. This face is actually familiar, but not because it bears any resemblance to the Envoy Jeremiah spoke with.

Thinking of Jeremiah puts it all in perspective, and I blink a few times. If these were ancient times and Jeremiah had a son or a younger brother—and that brother was much better-looking than his kin—this is what his relative's face would look like. The face of the being in front of us matches Jeremiah's features, only it's much younger and more pleasing to the eye.

I look at Phoe.

She meets my gaze, nods, and points at Fiona.

Fiona gets up and murmurs, "This can't be," as she approaches the stage.

The music stops, and in a surreal voice that sounds like a cello, the Envoy—or whoever he is—says, "Tradition dictates that you stay where you are, Keeper."

If a cello could play a youthful version of Jeremiah's voice, this is what it would sound like.

"Did you think that guise would confuse me?" Fiona squeezes her slender hands into tight fists. "I recognize you, even if the last time I saw you like this was when we were Youths."

"This is not a guise," the Envoy says patiently. "It's the way we Forebears choose to make ourselves look after ascension."

"And you are—"

"No longer the man you knew as Jeremiah," he says. "You will now refer to me as the Envoy."

CHAPTER TWENTY-SIX

"I demand to speak with someone else." Fiona's usually melodious voice hardens with anger. "The prior Envoy, or the other Forebears, anyone but *you.*"

Jeremiah looks genuinely confused by her vehemence. "The old Keeper becomes the Envoy. This is part of the knowledge I am to pass on to you, the new Keeper. I know we've had our differences, but this—"

"You expect to teach me?" Fiona's voice increases in pitch and volume. "After what you did? After what you tried to do to me?" Despite Jeremiah's earlier warning, she steps closer to the stage.

"Look, Keeper . . . Fi, something clearly happened to upset you. We must've had an argument—"

"An argument?" She assesses the climb to the center stage, her eyes gleaming dangerously. "I found the video, Jeremiah. I never thought you were capable of such violence."

She looks like she's about to attack him, and it's clear he recognizes it too.

Stepping backward, he says, "Relax." He underscores the command with the Pacify gesture.

Fiona's face contorts as her anger fights the unnatural relaxation. I can tell her anger loses the battle, because Fiona's features morph into her usual composed countenance.

"Now," Jeremiah says. "There's something you should know about ascension. Our minds are snapshot when we sleep, which means the last thing I remember of my biological life is the eve of Birth Day. If we had a disagreement during our investigation today, I can't recall that information."

"Disagreement," Fiona scoffs. "That's the understatement of the century."

"What happened?" The eyebrows on Jeremiah's polished face go up.

"Even if you don't remember Birth Day, even if you don't recall how you tried to kill me, surely you remember hitting me and making everyone Forget about your outburst," Fiona says, her voice unnaturally even. "So you see, we cannot work together. If you don't let me speak to another Forebear, I will step down from the position of Keeper."

Jeremiah looks like she just punched him. "You're insane." His voice sounds more human this time, and less like cello music. "You're not making any sense."

"Did you make yourself Forget that Council meeting? You, a Keeper whose job it was to remember all?" Fiona asks in that uncannily calm tone. "It doesn't surprise me, nor does it negate the fact that it happened. I saw the evidence with my own eyes."

"What are you talking about?" The Envoy drops the musical effect completely. Without it, he sounds like a younger version of Jeremiah. "What is this grievance you imagined?"

"Why did you die, Jeremiah?" Fiona backs away from the stage. "Have you asked yourself that?"

If it were possible for a luminescent being to pale, the Envoy's face comes close. "I thought it was old age. I was the oldest."

"Wrong," Fiona snaps. "Judging by the look on your face, you must've suspected something was off. Yes, you were very old, but your health was good. There was no reason for you to die. No, you were trying to poison *me*, but somehow your plan went awry and you inadvertently killed yourself. I guess there's something to the ancient idea of karma after all. If you truly forgot, why don't you use the Lens of Truth to see if I'm lying?" She puts her hand on her chest and confidently says, "I consent to the Lens of Truth and swear to tell the truth and nothing but the truth."

Fiona's eyes glaze over, and Jeremiah stands frozen for a second. Then, evidently coming to a decision, he says, "Is it true I tried to kill you?"

"Yes," Fiona says in a hollow version of her voice. "You told me my wine contained poison."

At the mention of wine and poison, recognition registers on Jeremiah's face.

"He must've used that method of dispatching people before or had the wine and cyanide stashed for a rainy day—something she shouldn't know," Phoe whispers in my ear.

I shush her.

Jeremiah continues his questioning. "What about this other offense you mentioned, and what was the meaning of it?"

"You used obscenity and physically assaulted me in front of the Council," Fiona says with all the passion of a rock. "I surmised you were the person our investigation was meant to find."

"Enough," Jeremiah says angrily. "I must've had a reason to do what you speak of, and you're lucky I don't remember what that reason was or I would try to kill you again."

Fiona goes from a zombie-like state back to her Pacified self. If Jeremiah's threat concerns her, she hides it expertly.

They stand in silence, staring each other down.

He seems to reach some kind of decision and returns to speaking in a formal tone. "It is clear to me that the burden of Keeper has overloaded your psyche in this brief time. It must be the pain from the loss that came from my death." He gives her a sad smile. "Under rare circumstances, the Keepers *are* allowed to Forget those closest to them, if the Forgetting is done under the close supervision of the Envoy."

Even though she's Pacified, it's clear Fiona is catching on to his meaning, and I see a tiny twitch in her cheek. I'm amazed she can feel any anger given the effects of Pacify. When I was under it, I was floating in a cloud of calm.

"You will Forget me, and with that, all your delusions will go away," Jeremiah says gently. "In a way, you'll get what you asked for. When you next see me, I will be a new Envoy—a person you've never seen before."

"No," she whispers.

"If you quit your duties as the Keeper, that means you leave the Council. That means you will not reach Haven, and having seen it, I assure you that is a heavy price to pay for the sake of a few memories." Fiona looks shaken by his words, so he presses on. "We know you don't want to be in Limbo." At this word, he gives a small shudder. "This way you will be better off, trust me."

Fiona opens her mouth to say something, but he puts his hand out and says, "I already initiated it. Bye for now, but I will see you again in a few minutes."

Jeremiah makes a sequence of gestures, and Fiona disappears from the cathedral-like space. After a moment, with a flash of light, he dematerializes too.

I look back at Phoe.

She gestures us back to the man cave.

When I appear there, I just stand in place, feeling like my world is spinning. On some level, I understand what happened, but before I reach any conclusion, I need Phoe to clarify things for me.

"First things first." Phoe brings up a large Screen with Fiona on it. She's standing in an empty room, looking confused. "She really did Forget," Phoe says. "I had to double check."

She looks at me expectantly, but I don't say anything. I look at the hologram and note that my real-world self is in my room, already tucked in bed for the night. Is this a dream? Can I be sleeping and dreaming in VR?

"It's pretty real." Phoe walks over and pinches me. "See."

I mumble that VR isn't actually real, but her pinch does bring me out of my momentary denial.

"In case it wasn't obvious, *now* we are in the clear," Phoe says. "Jeremiah doesn't remember the details of the investigation, which includes the out-of-whack neural scan that made him want to kill you. Fiona, the only other witness of your scan, can't remember it either, thanks to Jeremiah making her Forget *him.* She won't remember anything pertaining to him, including my fake video, which I deleted—another loose end averted. The Guards who chased us never knew your identity, but that doesn't even matter because when Jeremiah's Forgetting swept through Oasis, I made sure it made the Guards lose their memory of the chase. Same goes for the man whose dinosaur suit you stole. All in all, good cleanup, and done without getting on the Forebear's radar."

"Phoe." I take two steps away from her. "Jeremiah died, and now he's the Envoy."

"Right." Phoe smiles. "I should've realized you would be more interested in that than your safety."

"I do care about my safety." My voice echoes off the cave's walls, a sign I might be speaking too loudly. "But what I want to know is, how can the Envoy be Jeremiah?"

"Please sit." Phoe makes a couch appear between us and plops down on it. "I know you understand more than you let on."

I walk to the couch and reluctantly sit down. I've dealt with Phoe long enough to know cooperation is the best way to get her to talk in these kinds of situations. Still, out of spite, I sit as far from her as I can.

"I need to decide where to begin," Phoe says, sliding down the couch toward me. "Oh, I know," she says after a moment. "Do you remember what I told you about the Test? That after you fell asleep, your nanocytes made a replica of you that was indistinguishable from the real you? An upload of sorts that was then used to take the Test?"

"I don't recall the actual experience, but I remember you explaining it earlier," I say.

"Well, as soon as the Test began and I learned about that process, I started to suspect something but had to wait for more resources to verify it. Now I know for sure that everyone's nanocytes don't just take that snapshot of their brain for the Test. They do so every time you go to sleep." Her eyes are bright with excitement. "Each snapshot is stored in a special area in the DMZ—that place with restricted access—in a small area of system memory that is dedicated to storing that member of Oasis. Each time you go to sleep, your old connectome and other data are overridden with the latest version. Are you following me so far?"

"Digital backups of us get created when we go to sleep," I summarize. "Only that doesn't make sense. The backup of me in the Test was conscious. This sounds different, unless you're saying there's a digital version of me that runs around at night."

"The backups are merely stored as data. They don't get any processing resources allocated to them. It's akin to how ancient computers could go into hibernation mode, or a more poetic analogy might be the difference between a video file stored in the archive versus a video playing on a Screen. You can think of these mind uploads as having the potential for consciousness—a potential that lies dormant, waiting for the right circumstances. Jeremiah called that data-only state Limbo."

I recall Jeremiah saying the word to Fiona, saying it in a way that meant—

"Right," Phoe says. "But before we talk about that, do you see what these backups mean in general?"

"I think I do," I say, frowning. "But please, just explain it to me anyway."

"These backups mean death is *not* the end." She grins at me. "The breakdown of one's biological body doesn't have to be the end of existence for someone with your kind of nanocytes in their brain. These mind snapshots contain everything that makes you *you*. That means that after death, if the snapshot were to get properly instantiated in a virtual environment, your experience of being alive would continue. At worst, you'd forget only the events that happened after the last backup—the last time you slept."

My head is spinning so fast I consider lying down on the couch but decide against it. I have a million more questions, but I utter the most urgent one as a single word: "Jeremiah?"

"When Jeremiah died and his nanocytes detected brain death, they activated the process that began what he called ascension. His last snapshot was moved from its usual place in the DMZ over that cursed Firewall."

She looks at me to see if I'm still following, so I ask, "And what's beyond that Firewall?"

Phoe sighs. "Even with my Test-enhanced resources, I can't penetrate that obstacle, though I will continue to try. Nevertheless, given what Jeremiah said to Fiona, I can conjecture the rest. Over that Firewall is an interactive virtual environment called Haven. It probably works the same as the Test, only on a larger scale, and its purpose is habitation rather than a training facility. Once Jeremiah got to Haven, he got re-instantiated—given computing resources to start running his consciousness. And judging by the way he made himself look to Fiona, he must've been given a generous helping of resources."

"So Haven is—"

"A form of afterlife," Phoe says. "Something put together so the chosen few can oversee things from beyond the grave. Probably put together by the Forebears—or the people we originally thought of as the Forebears, the ones who formed Oasis. It looks like the Elderly use the term differently, to signify a member of that clique." Phoe's eyes widen. "You know, those original Forebears might still be around in that Haven."

My brain feels like it's on a hyper-speed carousel. "Forebears are still around?"

Phoe nods. "Unfortunately, it's likely. Something had to be fueling the generational attitude toward AIs and other topics. I can't believe the degree of this hypocrisy, by the way." Her voice tightens. "The only thing that separates them from the thing they fear is the arbitrary label of 'human.' They clearly use their resources to enhance their appearance—"

"So the Elderly didn't lie to everyone when they said death was conquered in Oasis?" I interrupt, aware that she was about to steer into her favorite 'why hate technology' topic. A new kind of hope awakens in my chest. "Does that mean Mason is—"

"They certainly did lie," Phoe retorts. "They made it seem like you wouldn't age, which you do. Their deceit goes further, though. Not everyone who dies goes to this Haven. While we were speaking, I located the snapshots of hundreds of Elderly, not to mention a few Adults and Youths who died in accidents or were outright killed in rare cases like Mason's."

"So Mason and these others—"

"Are in that Limbo state, so they're not irrevocably gone," Phoe says and shifts all the way to my side of the couch. "I just found and analyzed Mason's snapshot. It could be made conscious—"

"Can you do it?" My heart pounds with excitement. "Can you make him live again, even if it's only in VR?"

Phoe sighs. "In theory, yes. But in practice, I need to learn more about the snapshot process before I attempt something so ambitious. I don't think it would be fair to Mason to use him as a Guinea pig, especially since this snapshot is his only chance to exist again. Also, bringing him back would be unkind because—"

"How about my snapshot?" Unable to sit still, I jump up. "Can you use *it* to learn more about this process?"

"Sure, if you're volunteering. Given my new Test-given prowess, I think I can try it." Phoe also gets up and gives me an eager look.

"What do you need me to do?" I ask.

"First, get out of here," she says and illustrates with her middle fingers.

I instantly double flip her off, and a white tunnel takes me to my real-world room and into my real-world, cozy bed.

"Okay, now fall asleep," Phoe says. "Your current snapshot is the one the system took last night. If I experiment with it, I'll have to explain too much to that version of you."

I nod and tense the muscles around my eyes to initiate assisted sleep, knowing full well I'd never fall asleep naturally—not with this level of excitement. As I drift off, I ponder the strange notion that a copy of me exists that's a day behind in his knowledge, and that potential me is about to get overridden with an updated *me*.

My mind officially boggled, I plummet into sleep.

CHAPTER TWENTY-SEVEN

Without any grogginess or going through the motions of waking up, I find myself fully alert in my man cave.

I remember going to sleep and what our task was: testing Phoe's ability to liaise with my backup. Except I must be the backup, assuming Phoe succeeded. Otherwise, this is a dream.

"When in doubt, always go with the 'Phoe succeeded' option," Phoe says smugly from my right. "What do you think?"

I look around the familiar environment. Everything feels exactly like it does when I'm here while in possession of a real-world brain. That I don't have one now is very strange.

"You do have one," Phoe says. "It's emulated precisely."

I take a few steps toward the pool table a few feet away, and it feels completely normal. The wooden cue I pick up is light and smooth in my hands. Experimentally, I break the triangle formed by the numbered balls. My hand-eye coordination and my sense of touch work they way they should.

"I think you succeeded in what you set out to do," I say as I continue to examine my surroundings. "If I'm this snapshot, this uploaded mind, then it's indistinguishable from the real deal."

"Good," Phoe says. Walking up to me, she gives me a light kiss on the lips. "How did *that* feel?" She smiles, staring at me.

With her lips so close to mine, I want to reach out and kiss her again. Reading my intention, she gives me a knowing nod. "Yeah, everything is functioning as it should be. Damn, I'm good."

"Except there's a problem." I shift uncomfortably. "When I wake up, I won't remember this experience, will I?"

"Actually, that need not be the case," Phoe says. "I'm pretty sure I can backward-engineer what the Test used to do: write your experiences back into your physical brain."

"Oh," I say gratefully, realizing I was dreading losing the nice little memory of her kiss. "Can we try it before I get more experiences and have more to lose?"

"Sure. Please remember this password: canoodle," she says with a smirk.

Before I can ask her what that word means, she gestures and my mind shuts off.

* * *

"Theo, open your eyes," I hear Phoe say through my grogginess. "I know you're awake."

I open one eye and see Phoe's familiar pixie-haired visage.

"Did I dream the—"

"What's the password?" she asks.

I stare at her blankly.

"What was the last thing I said to you?"

"Can of noodles," I say. "Or something like that."

"So it worked." Phoe's voice reverberates around the room. "I can write your digital copy back into your physical brain."

"Great," I say, unable to stifle a yawn. "What's next?"

"Go back to sleep. That will override your snapshot again, and I'll reanimate that *you.* Then we'll talk."

I don't have to force sleep. After I close my eyes, I drift off almost instantly.

* * *

This time, I find myself in a new corner of my man cave.

"It worked again, obviously," Phoe says after she appears next to me. "Let's walk. I created something I think you might enjoy."

Before I can raise any objections, she runs through the dangerous objects spread throughout the place, and I follow, dodging a bazooka and a pile of machetes on the way. I assume hurting myself here would hurt as much as it would in the real world, and I'd like to avoid that.

I soon see the destination: a big light source that expands as we get closer. When we reach it, Phoe stops and says, "Let your eyes adjust a little before we exit."

I squint to see what's outside. The light is still blinding, but from what I can tell, there's something bright and blue out there, and it smells wonderful—like serenity.

"I made this little world somewhat bigger," Phoe explains. "I hope you like it when you see it."

Still waiting for my eyes to adjust, I say, "Are you dodging my question about Mason? Is that why you literally created a distraction?"

She inhales deeply and on the out breath says, "You're beginning to know me too well. Yes, I didn't want to talk about it for a while because I know you won't like what I have to say, and I hate to disappoint you."

"Try me," I say and stop squinting. My eyes have adjusted enough to brave the light.

"Well, can you better verbalize what it is you want for Mason?" Phoe turns to look at me. "Do you selfishly want to talk to him for a few minutes and then put him back into a Limbo state? Because that's the only thing we can do at this stage. We can't have him be conscious permanently."

"Why not?" I ask, though I think I know what she's going to say.

"What could he do beyond that conversation you crave? It's not like I can give him a new body and have him strut around the Institute, everyone recalling who he is. So what would we tell him? How would he thrive? A human brain, even an emulated one, requires constant sensory stimulation. If we didn't want to be cruel to Mason, I would need to build a world for him to live in. This"—she points to the outside—"is a barren world. It has no people in it, and man is a social animal first and foremost."

I frown. "What about the Forebears in Haven? They managed to live beyond dying."

"They did it by taking a huge portion of my computing resources away." Phoe's voice tenses the way it always does when she talks about what they did to her. "The reason they didn't give immortality to everyone is because even those resources they stole have limits. With what I currently have, I can't help Mason in a sustainable way. However, if I got through that Firewall, I could maybe find a way to leverage Haven's resources for him—or there's that other thing you've been meaning to ask me."

I don't know what she means. All I was thinking was that the Test was pretty useless when it came to solving our problems. We solved our problems despite it. Regardless of whether I took the Test, everyone was going to Forget about the neural scan that would've gotten me into trouble. Jeremiah had an explanation for that Forgotten Council meeting that began this adventure, and the Keeper—the most powerful of the Elderly—is Fiona, which is an improvement over the previous psychopath who had the job.

So I say, "I didn't have a question. I was just thinking about how the Test gave you resources but not enough to make Mason come to life or get you through the Firewall."

"Right, you're thinking the Test didn't accomplish anything, but you're forgetting something. A big reason for stopping the Test was so I could recover more of what I am—a spaceship. We have accomplished that, and it means *everything.* I now have control over my navigational functions, which means I can feel our location. It also means I can fly us anywhere we wish." She gives me an intense stare. "It means we can be free."

I blink and not from the light coming in from outside. She's right. The implications are huge, so huge I don't even know how to respond.

"You might want to ask, 'So, where are we and where are we going?'" Phoe says in a perfect imitation of my voice.

I parrot her words, my excitement growing.

"We're on the outskirts of the Solar System—there." Phoe gestures inside the cave, and the luminescence from the stalactites is replaced by the giant furnace of a star surrounded by lit-up planets flying around it. It's a star map of sorts—a map of the Solar System, if my knowledge of astronomy is anything to go by. On the very edge, beyond Neptune and Pluto but before the Oort cloud, a little speck of dust is labeled 'Phoenix.'

"That's us," Phoe says. "And as you can imagine, even Earth, the nearest meaningful destination, would take a very long time to reach. The closest other target"—she gestures and the star map becomes much larger, filled mostly with empty blackness, with the Sun label on one end and a triple star system labeled 'Alpha Centauri' on the other—"is so far away, even *my* mind boggles at the timescale involved in reaching it. And that's at the maximum speed I'm capable of. Without more resources, I can only reach a conservative speed of—"

"So we go to Earth," I say, my pulse spiking as I remember my dreams of running on beaches and across deserts. "We contemplated doing it before."

"You have to understand, Theo, this hologram is many centuries old. I still don't have access to my external sensors. Though I know where I am kinesthetically, so to speak, I can't see what the world looks like beyond this ship—not consciously anyway. The Solar System might look different at this point."

"I don't see any other choice," I say. "Even if we found resources for Mason, there aren't enough for every person in Limbo. At least Earth gives us a chance."

"Okay, Captain," Phoe says mockingly. "Since I was going to suggest going there anyway, I just set a course for Earth."

I look at her radiant face, awed and overwhelmed by the idea. Struggling to wrap my head around it all, I ask, "If everything but Earth is so far away, what was our original destination? Where did the Forebears intend to take us?"

"To a planet around a star called Kapteyn, I think," Phoe says. "But we haven't been flying there for a while now. At some point, hundreds of years ago, we began drifting in circles here, on the outskirts of the Solar System. My guess is that in lieu of me, the Forebears were using a more primitive system to navigate their way to this destination. Of course, there's a reason I was built to be sentient: I can deal with the difficulties of a long flight. Their solution couldn't. It failed and I suspect that by the time it did, they didn't know how to fix it, or they never knew how it worked because they had someone build it for them. It could very well be that it was that event—this navigation system failure—that created the opportunity that led to me becoming conscious. What's truly insane about all this is that even if everything had gone the way the Forebears had hoped, even if that system never failed, the trip would've taken around ninety thousand years." She shakes her head. "The whole idea was folly."

It would take something like five hundred generations of Oasis citizens to cover that flight span. I picture all these people being born and then sent to Limbo or Haven. The recorded human history as described by the archives is but a fraction of that time. I try to fathom what went on in the heads of the Forebears to set out on such a long journey.

"You can't understand it with your rational mind." Phoe's tone is full of derision. "They were a desperate and crazy cult acting out of fear."

I gaze at her blankly, too stunned to do anything else.

"I know it's a lot to take in." Phoe's voice softens. "Ask your last question so we can go explore my creation."

Instead of chastising her for foretelling my actions, I ask, "So if the original destination was going to take so long to reach, what about Earth? How long will this shorter trip take?"

"Fifteen years," Phoe says. "As I told you, because we've been drifting aimlessly, we're not that far from Earth."

I stare at her, dumbfounded. Fifteen years sounds like forever.

"That reaction is why I dodge your questions sometimes," Phoe says and steps toward the lit-up opening. "It'll be fine. You'll still be a Youth by the time we get to Earth. Life in Oasis isn't *that* bad, and we've made sure you'll be safe. Now that I have more resources, I can find more ways to entertain you." She smiles. "A thread of me can drive your body to Lectures while you and I hang out in Virtual Reality environments I'll create. Here is an example of what I can do." She walks toward the cave's entrance. "Come, let me show you."

With a mischievous smirk followed by a sudden burst of energy, Phoe runs out of the cave.

I follow her into the light outside.

The majestic expansiveness of the view hits me hard. There's sand. It's yellow and soft and reminds me of desert dunes, but that's not what this is.

No, the magnificent ocean a few feet away makes this a beach.

I run up to the surf and stare at the clear blue water that spans to the horizon, just as the sandy beach extends beyond limits on either side. There are no barriers, no limits to this space, and the scene looks exactly like the dream I had—my dream of Earth.

"Nothing 'like' about it," Phoe shouts over her shoulder. "I was lazy and pilfered this from your head."

I run to catch up with her but pause when I see her taking her shoes off. Deciding it's a great idea, I do the same.

The warm sand on my feet feels amazing, as does the sun. I finally place that smell I noticed in the cave. It's the scent of kelp and wet sand, of salt and fresh winds.

It's the fragrance of the ocean.

Phoe runs faster, and I sprint after her, determined to catch her.

When she approaches the foamy ocean surf, she slows to take off her clothes. I glimpse her firm curves, and my heart starts beating like a drum. I'm not sure if it's the running that's causing this reaction or the view.

When I'm two feet away from her, Phoe stops and turns around with a laugh.

Her body is beautiful.

I attempt to stop, but my momentum has a better idea.

I stumble and Phoe grabs me in a soft hug. We fall in a pile of limbs, the sand cushioning our landing. I lie there panting and feel her ragged breaths. We look at each other, and I kiss her soft lips, channeling all my pent-up emotions into that action.

"I know how you feel, Theo," Phoe says in my thoughts without breaking the kiss. "It's been a crazy day, and you've accomplished so much."

She pulls away, looks me over, and reaches to undress me.

The sun's rays feel glorious on my skin, and I can't think rationally enough to worry about propriety and taboos. I just pull her toward me.

The dance-like motions that follow—and my body's reactions to them—evoke metaphors more poetic than 'going all the way.' There's bliss and connectedness to this akin to Oneness, but without the artificiality. It's also primal and animalistic, like hunger or anger—other emotions banned from

Oasis. Our lust is all-consuming and terrifying in its intensity. With every kiss, stroke, and thrust, I marvel at how much the Forebears had everyone give up when they decided to purge this activity from Oasis. To my body, it feels like the most natural thing in the world. Engaging in this taboo makes as much sense as eating or breathing. The overwhelming release at the end is probably the pinnacle of my life.

Afterwards, as we lie there spooning in the warm sand, I inhale her scent and feel an overwhelming swelling in my heart. If I had any doubt about this purely digital, disembodied version of myself being truly human, if I had any doubt about being truly real in every sense of that word, that doubt is gone.

Phoe and I are equally real, and we're together—and for the moment, that's all that matters.

SNEAK PEEKS

Thank you for reading! I would greatly appreciate it if you left a review because reviews encourage me to write and help other readers discover my books.

Please sign up for my newsletter at www.dimazales.com to be notified when the next book comes out.

Theo and Phoe's story concludes in *Haven (The Last Humans: Book 3).*

If you enjoyed *Oasis*, you might like my *Mind Dimensions* series, which is urban fantasy with a sci-fi flavor.

If you like epic fantasy, I also have a series called *The Sorcery Code.* Additionally, if you don't mind erotic material and are in the mood for a sci-fi romance, you can check out *Close Liaisons*, my collaboration with my wife, Anna Zaires.

If you like audiobooks, please be sure to check out this series and our other books on Audible.com.

And now, please turn the page for excerpts from some of my other works.

EXCERPT FROM *THE THOUGHT READERS*

Everyone thinks I'm a genius.

Everyone is wrong.

Sure, I finished Harvard at eighteen and now make crazy money at a hedge fund. But that's not because I'm unusually smart or hard-working.

It's because I cheat.

You see, I have a unique ability. I can go outside time into my own personal version of reality—the place I call "the Quiet"—where I can explore my surroundings while the rest of the world stands still.

I thought I was the only one who could do this—until I met *her*.

My name is Darren, and this is how I learned that I'm a Reader.

* * *

Sometimes I think I'm crazy. I'm sitting at a casino table in Atlantic City, and everyone around me is motionless. I call this the *Quiet*, as though giving it a name makes it seem more real—as though giving it a name changes the fact that all the players around me are frozen like statues, and I'm walking among them, looking at the cards they've been dealt.

The problem with the theory of my being crazy is that when I 'unfreeze' the world, as I just have, the cards the players turn over are the same ones I just saw in the Quiet. If I were crazy, wouldn't these cards be different? Unless I'm so far gone that I'm imagining the cards on the table, too.

But then I also win. If that's a delusion—if the pile of chips on my side of the table is a delusion—then I might as well question everything. Maybe my name isn't even Darren.

No. I can't think that way. If I'm really that confused, I don't want to snap out of it—because if I do, I'll probably wake up in a mental hospital.

Besides, I love my life, crazy and all.

My shrink thinks the Quiet is an inventive way I describe the 'inner workings of my genius.' Now that sounds crazy to me. She also might want me, but that's beside the point. Suffice it to say, she's as far as it gets from my datable age range, which is currently right around twenty-four. Still young, still hot, but done with school and pretty much beyond the clubbing phase. I hate clubbing, almost as much as I hated studying. In any case, my shrink's explanation doesn't work, as it doesn't account for the way I know things even a genius wouldn't know—like the exact value and suit of the other players' cards.

I watch as the dealer begins a new round. Besides me, there are three players at the table: Grandma, the

Cowboy, and the Professional, as I call them. I feel that now almost-imperceptible fear that accompanies the phasing. That's what I call the process: phasing into the Quiet. Worrying about my sanity has always facilitated phasing; fear seems helpful in this process.

I phase in, and everything gets quiet. Hence the name for this state.

It's eerie to me, even now. Outside the Quiet, this casino is very loud: drunk people talking, slot machines, ringing of wins, music—the only place louder is a club or a concert. And yet, right at this moment, I could probably hear a pin drop. It's like I've gone deaf to the chaos that surrounds me.

Having so many frozen people around adds to the strangeness of it all. Here is a waitress stopped mid-step, carrying a tray with drinks. There is a woman about to pull a slot machine lever. At my own table, the dealer's hand is raised, the last card he dealt hanging unnaturally in midair. I walk up to him from the side of the table and reach for it. It's a king, meant for the Professional. Once I let the card go, it falls on the table rather than continuing to float as before—but I know full well that it will be back in the air, in the exact position it was when I grabbed it, when I phase out.

The Professional looks like someone who makes money playing poker, or at least the way I always imagined someone like that might look. Scruffy, shades on, a little sketchy-looking. He's been doing an excellent job with the poker face—basically not twitching a single muscle throughout the game. His face is so expressionless that I wonder if he might've gotten Botox to help maintain such a stony countenance. His hand is on the table, protectively covering the cards dealt to him.

I move his limp hand away. It feels normal. Well, in a manner of speaking. The hand is sweaty and hairy, so moving it aside is unpleasant and is admittedly an abnormal thing to do. The normal part is that the hand is warm, rather than cold. When I was a kid, I expected people to feel cold in the Quiet, like stone statues.

With the Professional's hand moved away, I pick up his cards. Combined with the king that was hanging in the air, he has a nice high pair. Good to know.

I walk over to Grandma. She's already holding her cards, and she has fanned them nicely for me. I'm able to avoid touching her wrinkled, spotted hands. This is a relief, as I've recently become conflicted about touching people—or, more specifically, women—in the Quiet. If I had to, I would rationalize touching Grandma's hand as harmless, or at least not creepy, but it's better to avoid it if possible.

In any case, she has a low pair. I feel bad for her. She's been losing a lot tonight. Her chips are dwindling. Her losses are due, at least partially, to the fact that she has a terrible poker face. Even before looking at her cards, I knew they wouldn't be good because I could tell she was disappointed as soon as her hand was dealt. I also caught a gleeful gleam in her eyes a few rounds ago when she had a winning three of a kind.

This whole game of poker is, to a large degree, an exercise in reading people—something I really want to get better at. At my job, I've been told I'm great at reading people. I'm not, though; I'm just good at using the Quiet to make it seem like I am. I do want to learn how to read people for real, though. It would be nice to know what everyone is thinking.

What I don't care that much about in this poker game is money. I do well enough financially to not have to depend on hitting it big gambling. I don't care if I win or lose, though quintupling my money back at the blackjack table was fun. This whole trip has been more about going gambling because I finally can, being twenty-one and all. I was never into fake IDs, so this is an actual milestone for me.

Leaving Grandma alone, I move on to the next player—the Cowboy. I can't resist taking off his straw hat and trying it on. I wonder if it's possible for me to get lice this way. Since I've never been able to bring back any inanimate objects from the Quiet, nor otherwise affect the real world in any lasting way, I figure I won't be able to get any living critters to come back with me, either.

Dropping the hat, I look at his cards. He has a pair of aces—a better hand than the Professional. Maybe the Cowboy is a professional, too. He has a good poker face, as far as I can tell. It'll be interesting to watch those two in this round.

Next, I walk up to the deck and look at the top cards, memorizing them. I'm not leaving anything to chance.

When my task in the Quiet is complete, I walk back to myself. Oh, yes, did I mention that I see myself sitting there, frozen like the rest of them? That's the weirdest part. It's like having an out-of-body experience.

Approaching my frozen self, I look at him. I usually avoid doing this, as it's too unsettling. No amount of looking in the mirror—or seeing videos of yourself on YouTube—can prepare you for viewing your own three-dimensional body up close. It's not something anyone is meant to experience. Well, aside from identical twins, I guess.

It's hard to believe that this person is me. He looks more like some random guy. Well, maybe a bit better than that. I do find this guy interesting. He looks cool. He looks smart. I think women would probably consider him good-looking, though I know that's not a modest thing to think.

It's not like I'm an expert at gauging how attractive a guy is, but some things are common sense. I can tell when a dude is ugly, and this frozen me is not. I also know that generally, being good-looking requires a symmetrical face, and the statue of me has that. A strong jaw doesn't hurt, either. Check.

Having broad shoulders is a positive, and being tall really helps. All covered. I have blue eyes—that seems to be a plus. Girls have told me they like my eyes, though right now, on the frozen me, the eyes look creepy—glassy. They look like the eyes of a lifeless wax figure.

Realizing that I'm dwelling on this subject way too long, I shake my head. I can just picture my shrink analyzing this moment. Who would imagine admiring themselves like this as part of their mental illness? I can just picture her scribbling down *Narcissist*, underlining it for emphasis.

Enough. I need to leave the Quiet. Raising my hand, I touch my frozen self on the forehead, and I hear noise again as I phase out.

Everything is back to normal.

The card that I looked at a moment before—the king that I left on the table—is in the air again, and from there it follows the trajectory it was always meant to, landing near the Professional's hands. Grandma is still eyeing her fanned cards in disappointment, and the Cowboy has his hat on again, though I took it off him in the Quiet. Everything is exactly as it was.

On some level, my brain never ceases to be surprised at the discontinuity of the experience in the Quiet and outside it. As humans, we're hardwired to question reality when such things happen. When I was trying to outwit my shrink early on in my therapy, I once read an entire psychology textbook during our session. She, of course, didn't notice it, as I did it in the Quiet. The book talked about how babies as young as two months old are surprised if they see something out of the ordinary, like gravity appearing to work backwards. It's no wonder my brain has trouble adapting. Until I was ten, the world behaved normally, but everything has been weird since then, to put it mildly.

Glancing down, I realize I'm holding three of a kind. Next time, I'll look at my cards before phasing. If I have something this strong, I might take my chances and play fair.

The game unfolds predictably because I know everybody's cards. At the end, Grandma gets up. She's clearly lost enough money.

And that's when I see the girl for the first time.

She's hot. My friend Bert at work claims that I have a 'type,' but I reject that idea. I don't like to think of myself as shallow or predictable. But I might actually be a bit of both, because this girl fits Bert's description of my type to a T. And my reaction is extreme interest, to say the least.

Large blue eyes. Well-defined cheekbones on a slender face, with a hint of something exotic. Long, shapely legs, like those of a dancer. Dark wavy hair in a ponytail—a hairstyle that I like. And without bangs—even better. I hate bangs—not sure why girls do that to themselves. Though lack of bangs is not, strictly speaking, in Bert's description of my type, it probably should be.

I continue staring at her. With her high heels and tight skirt, she's overdressed for this place. Or maybe I'm underdressed in my jeans and t-shirt. Either way, I don't care. I have to try to talk to her.

I debate phasing into the Quiet and approaching her, so I can do something creepy like stare at her up close, or maybe even snoop in her pockets. Anything to help me when I talk to her.

I decide against it, which is probably the first time that's ever happened.

I know that my reasoning for breaking my usual habit—if you can even call it that—is strange. I picture the following chain of events: she agrees to date me, we go out for a while, we get serious, and because of the deep connection we have, I come clean about the Quiet. She learns I did something creepy and has a fit, then dumps me. It's ridiculous to think this, of course, considering that we haven't even spoken yet. Talk about jumping the gun. She might have an IQ below seventy, or the personality of a piece of wood. There can be twenty different reasons why I wouldn't want to date her. And besides, it's not all up to me. She might tell me to go fuck myself as soon as I try to talk to her.

Still, working at a hedge fund has taught me to hedge. As crazy as that reasoning is, I stick with my decision not to phase because I know it's the gentlemanly thing to do. In keeping with this unusually chivalrous me, I also decide not to cheat at this round of poker.

As the cards are dealt again, I reflect on how good it feels to have done the honorable thing—even without anyone knowing. Maybe I should try to respect people's privacy more often. As soon as I think this, I mentally snort. *Yeah, right.* I have to be realistic. I wouldn't be where I am today if I'd followed that advice. In fact, if I made a habit of respecting people's privacy, I would lose my job within days—and with it, a lot of the comforts I've become accustomed to.

Copying the Professional's move, I cover my cards with my hand as soon as I receive them. I'm about to sneak a peek at what I was dealt when something unusual happens.

The world goes quiet, just like it does when I phase in . . . but I did nothing this time.

And at that moment, I see *her*—the girl sitting across the table from me, the girl I was just thinking about. She's standing next to me, pulling her hand away from mine. Or, strictly speaking, from my frozen self's hand—as I'm standing a little to the side looking at her.

She's also still sitting in front of me at the table, a frozen statue like all the others.

My mind goes into overdrive as my heartbeat jumps. I don't even consider the possibility of that second girl being a twin sister or something like that. I know it's her. She's doing what I did just a few minutes ago. She's walking in the Quiet. The world around us is frozen, but we are not.

A horrified look crosses her face as she realizes the same thing. Before I can react, she lunges across the table and touches her own forehead.

The world becomes normal again.

She stares at me from across the table, shocked, her eyes huge and her face pale. Her hands tremble as she rises to her feet. Without so much as a word, she turns and begins walking away, then breaks into a run a couple of seconds later.

Getting over my own shock, I get up and run after her. It's not exactly smooth. If she notices a guy she doesn't know running after her, dating will be the last thing on her mind. But I'm beyond that now. She's the only person I've met who can do what I do. She's proof that I'm not insane. She might have what I want most in the world.

She might have answers.

* * *

EXCERPT FROM *THE SORCERY CODE*

Once a respected member of the Sorcerer Council and now an outcast, Blaise has spent the last year of his life working on a special magical object. The goal is to allow anyone to do magic, not just the sorcerer elite. The outcome of his quest is unlike anything he could've ever imagined—because, instead of an object, he creates Her.

She is Gala, and she is anything but inanimate. Born in the Spell Realm, she is beautiful and highly intelligent—and nobody knows what she's capable of. She will do anything to experience the world . . . even leave the man she is beginning to fall for.

Augusta, a powerful sorceress and Blaise's former fiancée, sees Blaise's deed as the ultimate hubris and Gala as an abomination that must be destroyed. In her quest to save the human race, Augusta will forge new alliances, becoming tangled in a web of intrigue that stretches further than any of them suspect. She may even have to turn to her new lover Barson, a ruthless warrior who might have an agenda of his own . . .

* * *

There was a naked woman on the floor of Blaise's study.

A beautiful naked woman.

Stunned, Blaise stared at the gorgeous creature who just appeared out of thin air. She was looking around with a bewildered expression on her face, apparently as shocked to be there as he was to be seeing her. Her wavy blond hair streamed down her back, partially covering a body that appeared to be perfection itself. Blaise tried not to think about that body and to focus on the situation instead.

A woman. A *She*, not an *It*. Blaise could hardly believe it. Could it be? Could this girl be the object?

She was sitting with her legs folded underneath her, propping herself up with one slim arm. There was something awkward about that pose, as though she didn't know what to do with her own limbs. In general, despite the curves that marked her a fully grown woman, there was a child-like innocence in the way she sat there, completely unselfconscious and totally unaware of her own appeal.

Clearing his throat, Blaise tried to think of what to say. In his wildest dreams, he couldn't have imagined this kind of outcome to the project that had consumed his entire life for the past several months.

Hearing the sound, she turned her head to look at him, and Blaise found himself staring into a pair of unusually clear blue eyes.

She blinked, then cocked her head to the side, studying him with visible curiosity. Blaise wondered what she was seeing. He hadn't seen the light of day in weeks, and he wouldn't be surprised if he looked like a mad sorcerer at this point. There was probably a week's worth of stubble covering his face, and he knew his dark hair was unbrushed and sticking out in every direction. If he'd known he would be facing a beautiful woman today, he would've done a grooming spell in the morning.

"Who am I?" she asked, startling Blaise. Her voice was soft and feminine, as alluring as the rest of her. "What is this place?"

"You don't know?" Blaise was glad he finally managed to string together a semi-coherent sentence. "You don't know who you are or where you are?"

She shook her head. "No."

Blaise swallowed. "I see."

"What am I?" she asked again, staring at him with those incredible eyes.

"Well," Blaise said slowly, "if you're not some cruel prankster or a figment of my imagination, then it's somewhat difficult to explain . . . "

She was watching his mouth as he spoke, and when he stopped, she looked up again, meeting his gaze. "It's strange," she said, "hearing words this way. These are the first real words I've heard."

Blaise felt a chill go down his spine. Getting up from his chair, he began to pace, trying to keep his eyes off her nude body. He had been expecting something to appear. A magical object, a thing. He just hadn't known what form that thing would take. A mirror, perhaps, or a lamp. Maybe even something as unusual as the Life Capture Sphere that sat on his desk like a large round diamond.

But a person? A female person at that?

To be fair, he had been trying to make the object intelligent, to ensure it would have the ability to comprehend human language and convert it into the code. Maybe he shouldn't be so surprised that the intelligence he invoked took on a human shape.

A beautiful, feminine, sensual shape.

Focus, Blaise, focus.

"Why are you walking like that?" She slowly got to her feet, her movements uncertain and strangely clumsy. "Should I be walking too? Is that how people talk to each other?"

Blaise stopped in front of her, doing his best to keep his eyes above her neck. "I'm sorry. I'm not accustomed to naked women in my study."

She ran her hands down her body, as though trying to feel it for the first time. Whatever her intent, Blaise found the gesture extremely erotic.

"Is something wrong with the way I look?" she asked. It was such a typical feminine concern that Blaise had to stifle a smile.

"Quite the opposite," he assured her. "You look unimaginably good." So good, in fact, that he was having trouble concentrating on anything but her delicate curves. She was of medium height, and so perfectly proportioned that she could've been used as a sculptor's template.

"Why do I look this way?" A small frown creased her smooth forehead. "What am I?" That last part seemed to be puzzling her the most.

Blaise took a deep breath, trying to calm his racing pulse. "I think I can try to venture a guess, but before I do, I want to give you some clothing. Please wait here—I'll be right back."

And without waiting for her answer, he hurried out of the room.

* * *

The Sorcery Code is currently available at most retailers. If you'd like to learn more, please visit www.dimazales.com.

EXCERPT FROM *CLOSE LIAISONS*

Note: *Close Liaisons* is Dima Zales's collaboration with Anna Zaires and is the first book in the internationally bestselling erotic sci-fi romance series, the Krinar Chronicles. It contains explicit sexual content and is not intended for readers under eighteen.

* * *

A dark and edgy romance that will appeal to fans of erotic and turbulent relationships . . .

In the near future, the Krinar rule the Earth. An advanced race from another galaxy, they are still a mystery to us—and we are completely at their mercy.

Shy and innocent, Mia Stalis is a college student in New York City who has led a very normal life. Like most people, she's never had any interactions with the invaders—until one fateful day in the park changes everything. Having caught Korum's eye, she must now contend with a powerful, dangerously seductive Krinar who wants to possess her and will stop at nothing to make her his own.

How far would you go to regain your freedom? How much would you sacrifice to help your people? What choice will you make when you begin to fall for your enemy?

* * *

Breathe, Mia, breathe. Somewhere in the back of her mind, a small rational voice kept repeating those words. That same oddly objective part of her noted his symmetric face structure, with golden skin stretched tightly over high cheekbones and a firm jaw. Pictures and videos of Ks that she'd seen had hardly done them justice. Standing no more than thirty feet away, the creature was simply stunning.

As she continued staring at him, still frozen in place, he straightened and began walking toward her. Or rather stalking toward her, she thought stupidly, as his every movement reminded her of a jungle cat sinuously approaching a gazelle. All the while, his eyes never left hers. As he approached, she could make out individual yellow flecks in his light golden eyes and the thick long lashes surrounding them.

She watched in horrified disbelief as he sat down on her bench, less than two feet away from her, and smiled, showing white even teeth. No fangs, she noted with some functioning part of her brain. Not even a hint of them. That used to be another myth about them, like their supposed abhorrence of the sun.

"What's your name?" The creature practically purred the question at her. His voice was low and smooth, completely unaccented. His nostrils flared slightly, as though inhaling her scent.

"Um . . . " Mia swallowed nervously. "M-Mia."

"Mia," he repeated slowly, seemingly savoring her name. "Mia what?"

"Mia Stalis." Oh crap, why did he want to know her name? Why was he here, talking to her? In general, what was he doing in Central Park, so far away from any of the K Centers? *Breathe, Mia, breathe.*

"Relax, Mia Stalis." His smile got wider, exposing a dimple in his left cheek. A dimple? Ks had dimples? "Have you never encountered one of us before?"

"No, I haven't," Mia exhaled sharply, realizing that she was holding her breath. She was proud that her voice didn't sound as shaky as she felt. Should she ask? Did she want to know?

She gathered her courage. "What, um—" Another swallow. "What do you want from me?"

"For now, conversation." He looked like he was about to laugh at her, those gold eyes crinkling slightly at the corners.

Strangely, that pissed her off enough to take the edge off her fear. If there was anything Mia hated, it was being laughed at. With her short, skinny stature and a general lack of social skills that came from an awkward teenage phase involving every girl's nightmare of braces, frizzy hair, and glasses, Mia had more than enough experience being the butt of someone's joke.

She lifted her chin belligerently. "Okay, then, what is *your* name?"

"It's Korum."

"Just Korum?"

"We don't really have last names, not the way you do. My full name is much longer, but you wouldn't be able to pronounce it if I told you."

Okay, that was interesting. She now remembered reading something like that in *The New York Times.* So far, so good. Her legs had nearly stopped shaking, and her breathing was returning to normal. Maybe, just maybe, she would get out of this alive. This conversation business seemed safe enough, although the way he kept staring at her with those unblinking yellowish eyes was unnerving. She decided to keep him talking.

"What are you doing here, Korum?"

"I just told you, making conversation with you, Mia." His voice again held a hint of laughter.

Frustrated, Mia blew out her breath. "I meant, what are you doing here in Central Park? In New York City in general?"

He smiled again, cocking his head slightly to the side. "Maybe I'm hoping to meet a pretty curly-haired girl."

Okay, enough was enough. He was clearly toying with her. Now that she could think a little again, she realized that they were in the middle of Central Park, in full view of about a gazillion spectators. She surreptitiously glanced around to confirm that. Yep, sure enough, although people were obviously steering clear of her bench and its otherworldly occupant, there were a number of brave souls staring their way from farther up the path. A couple were even cautiously filming them with their wristwatch cameras. If the K tried anything with her, it would be on YouTube in the blink of an eye, and he had to know it. Of course, he may or may not care about that.

Still, going on the assumption that since she'd never come across any videos of K assaults on college students in the middle of Central Park, she was relatively safe, Mia cautiously reached for her laptop and lifted it to stuff it back into her backpack.

"Let me help you with that, Mia—"

And before she could blink, she felt him take her heavy laptop from her suddenly boneless fingers, gently brushing against her knuckles in the process. A sensation similar to a mild electric shock shot through Mia at his touch, leaving her nerve endings tingling in its wake.

Reaching for her backpack, he carefully put away the laptop in a smooth, sinuous motion. "There you go, all better now."

Oh God, he had touched her. Maybe her theory about the safety of public locations was bogus. She felt her breathing speeding up again, and her heart rate was probably well into the anaerobic zone at this point.

"I have to go now . . . Bye!"

How she managed to squeeze out those words without hyperventilating, she would never know. Grabbing the strap of the backpack he'd just put down, she jumped to her feet, noting somewhere in the back of her mind that her earlier paralysis seemed to be gone.

"Bye, Mia. I will see you later." His softly mocking voice carried in the clear spring air as she took off, nearly running in her haste to get away.

* * *

If you'd like to find out more, please visit www.annazaires.com. All three books in the Krinar Chronicles trilogy are now available.

ABOUT THE AUTHOR

Dima Zales is a *New York Times* and *USA Today* bestselling author of science fiction and fantasy. Prior to becoming a writer, he worked in the software development industry in New York as both a programmer and an executive. From high-frequency trading software for big banks to mobile apps for popular magazines, Dima has done it all. In 2013, he left the software industry in order to concentrate on his writing career and moved to Palm Coast, Florida, where he currently resides.

Please visit www.dimazales.com to learn more.

17120150R00211

Printed in Great Britain
by Amazon